YEAR OF THE RAT

Ridley McIntyre

Published by Suburban Legend.
Copyright © 2023 Ridley McIntyre

ISBN: 0-9984265-0-4
ISBN-13: 978-0-9984265-0-1

First Edition.

An earlier version of "Boy" appeared in the March/April 1992 edition of InterText Magazine.
An earlier version of "Monkeytrick" appeared in the July/August 1994 edition of InterText Magazine.
An earlier version of "Ghostdancer" appeared in the September/October 1995 edition of InterText Magazine.

For more information about the author, Ridley McIntyre, please visit ridski.com

Special thanks to my enablers
Jason Snell and Antony Johnston.
Much gratitude also goes out to David, Steve,
Mark and Charlie: the original Harlequins.

For Chrissy, who believed.

PART ONE

BOY

CHAPTER ONE

"If it's the wrong place and the wrong time, I'll be there." — Big Pierrot

Shi Zhongxin. The Manhattan Outzone. The Year of the Rat.

A hot midnight rainstorm washes the busy streets of the Outzone. A decade ago, The New Atlantic City Metropolitan Authority declared much of the city too expensive to police. They left the running of the place to various corporate factions and their surrogate gangs, or Tag Teams. Every month, the Tag Teams fight against each other in a televised cybernetically-enhanced mixed martial arts tournament. Team Huawei, last month's victors, run the streets but keep things loose and fun here in Shi Zhongxin as long as you don't cross swords with them, and Boy Eastman has every intention of staying under their radar.

He lets the camera scan his ID and steps through the metal detector of Team Huawei's main dance club, Snakestrike, on East 7th Street. In daylight, high above the doors you can still read the words "Cooper Union" and "To Science And Art" even further up the main walls. Someone had said that the building had stood there for over 200 years, surviving Black November, the Crash that followed, and the riots and wars that came after that. It seemed fitting then, that after all the shit that this building's seen, it would be the perfect place to hold a non-stop party.

Snakestrike's DJ tonight is a tiger-haired maestro. One of the few in the world who can keep up with the countless samples, loops, and basslines flowing from the software in his head while simultaneously rapping in Cantonese and hyping the mostly teenage crowd before him. He is engrossed in the world of the music, every digitized blip and beep and thump pulsing through his nerves like the very blood in his veins. Electrical signals interfacing the sound system to his nervous system allow him complete control over the mix.

The dance floor is swarming, blue laser beams reflecting off their faces, fluorescent gloves pulsing under the ultra-violet strobes. Every wall of the club writhes with holographic snake scales, a reptilian world of perpetual motion.

There's a mezzanine above the dance floor where people from the level above can watch the dancers. Up here, on the left at the cocktail bar, Snakestrike stinks of sweat and business. And while Boy came for the business, the only thing greasing his palms is sweat.

Two women serve the cocktail bar. One is dark-haired with the body and grace of a ballet dancer, the other a half-Japanese bottle blonde who moonlights as a cheerleader for Team Huawei. They're faking interest in a drunk Panasony wageslave who is trying to convince them he's a big-spending important Regional Vice President despite his wageslave haircut and his wageslave work boots. Boy watches them gaming each other with interest, then catches the attention of the dark-haired girl over to order a tequila.

Boy is here to see Laughing Simon, Team Huawei's best

engineer, but Laughing Simon's notoriety for forgetting appointments proves to be well-deserved, even though Boy messaged the engineer's slug about five times. So he sits by the bar with his face cupped in his hand and a pocketful of kerndrives filled with pleasure-center stimulant softs in his black pilot's jacket. He is just thinking of leaving when he feels a tap on his shoulder from the billy on the grey stool next to him: a muscular Australian kid with sideburns, a blue denim jacket, hair at an improbable angle, and a strawberry-blond mustache.

"So what do you do?" asks the billy.

"Are you collecting taxes or hitting on me?" Boy answers in an English accent.

The dark-haired girl returns with a plastic tumbler wondering if there are any Americans left in Shi Zhongxin, then smiles at that irony. Shi Zhongxin was a haven for expats from all over the globe. Besides, how many Americans would hang out in a neighborhood they could barely pronounce? She pours the tequila and Boy throws the liquid down his throat like it had escaped a jail.

"You look like a ghost to me," says the Australian.

Boy shakes his head the way he's supposed to when they ask him these questions. For a ghost, he sure seemed visible. "Sorry, ace. I'm just your everyday pony."

The billy shuffles closer, his voice slipping gently into a business tone. "Shame. I'm looking for some hot paydata and I really need a ghost. One of the best. Someone like Camden Town Boy. Boy Eastman."

"You've found Boy Eastman, ace. But I gave up the ghost over a year ago."

The billy makes a swift move from his jacket and Boy can feel a cold plastic tube dig into his hip. The Australian raises his eyebrows. "Looks like I've found my man, then." He motions to the exit with his head. "We're walking."

"You're walking. I'm drinking."

The Australian squints in Boy's face. "You'd better move, 'cause if you don't I'm gonna spray your brains all over this bar."

Boy sits still. "I've been in this bar listening to Cantonese pop music for the best part of 10 minutes and under those circumstances the choice of leaving or having my brains blown out would fill me with joy no matter what happened. But, and this is not a warning but a promise, if you touch that trigger you won't get out of here alive. They like me here. I'm a likable guy. You, however, have violated the golden rule of this club." A flick of Boy's eyes motions the Australian to look at the dark-haired bargirl. She holds the assault shotgun usually kept under the bar. Casually, and with a feisty smile, she rests the double-barrel on the bone of the Australian's nose and crunches the first two rounds into the chamber.

"16 shot, pump action, double-barrel repeater. If you're takin' anyone out at my bar, it won't be with a plastic pistol, sport," she says curtly. "Give me that piece of shit and deal with the man friendly-like."

The Australian gives over the gun with a taut look from Boy to the bargirl and back. He wipes sweat from his mustache.

Boy gives a thankful look to the bargirl. "Xiexie," he says, even though he knows his intonation is way off the mark. His Chinese is improving and he tries to practice it wherever he can.

"He's lucky he's so dumb-looking," she replies, "otherwise I'd shoot him anyway." She puts the guns behind the counter, out of reach, and goes back to the flirting with the wageslave for the tips she knows he can't afford.

Boy turns to the Australian. "You've got two minutes. Deal or step."

The billy talks through clenched teeth. "My name's Priest.

I'm a dealer for Kreskin."

"Anatoly Kreskin? Mister Fixit?"

"The very same. Kreskin says you two used to work together. You used to do Russian laundry for him."

"Funny you should say that I read a rumor that I set up a couple of microfinancing companies for him in exchange for a motorcycle. Completely untrue, of course, and even if it was, I was well-compensated and we should be favor-neutral by now."

"Yeah, well, there's been a bird flu outbreak in Seattle. Kreskin has a deal with one of the hospitals to supply vaccines, and he has a ton of them, but Madoka's passage fees just went through the roof. He wants to send some viajeros over the Corn Road, but he's coming up against some tough gunship opposition and he needs you to run the interface for him. Break into the Madoka Farms shell and find out the reconnaissance flight plans for next week." He pauses for effect and sighs. "Obviously, we could ship through Canada, but the Corn Road's more direct. He says you did it before for him. He says you'll do it again."

Boy narrows his eyes. "Read my profile. Ex-ghost."

Priest smiles. "Kreskin said you'd be a little reluctant. I have read your profile. Ex-ghost. Ex-Madoka software engineer. Ex-viajero. One more 'ex' and you've got a team of mutant superheroes. It's a heck of a resume for a kid." Priest leans in, his face opening, trying to look friendly. It's the face of a salesman reaching the end of his pitch. "Look, Boy, Kreskin needs someone he can trust. Someone he knows. And of course, if you refuse…" Priest takes a cold gyoza dumpling from a bowl on the bar and bites half of it.

"Kreskin publicly announces my whereabouts to Madoka."

"I think he had something even worse in mind, but you're on the right track. Strictly business, you understand, Boy. Nothing personal."

Somehow Boy wishes it was personal. Then he'd have an excuse to smash Priest's face in.

CHAPTER TWO

"Sometimes you just gotta get your halo dirty." —
Big Pierrot.

Kitty slips into Boy's room and hands him steaming ration coffee in a polystyrene cup. She's like him, another smart young refugee from the authorities. The Manhattan Outzone is an excellent place to hide, but she was born a farm girl, not a city rat, and no one can hide forever.

She looks at Boy through shiny Panasony eyes as he drinks coffee and fidgets in his black leather office chair, and she realizes that she knows very little about him. He grew up in Pancras Wells, a shanty town in the Thames Midland Metroplex, and found a way out through running the interface; Camden Town Boy. He was a legend among the ghosts of the old internet by the age of fourteen, teaching others like Dagger and Man Friday to run the interface, data mining, money-skimming, and identity stealing. He had become a name, and names are bad in a world where you need to be anonymous to survive.

At fifteen he was involved in a gang rivalry squabble and left for the States. There he faked a new identity and got a job with Madoka Farms which owns all the good land from the Ohio Valley to the Rockies, hoping the corporation's tight security would be enough to protect his whereabouts. There he remained for a year, monitoring a squadron of auto-security drones. Sometimes, he had told her, he even got a chance to pilot one himself.

Madoka's biggest enemy, apart from Mother Nature herself, were the Viajeros - travelers or nomads, who had dropped off the grid and scratched a living smuggling weapons, drugs, black data, and all that fun stuff from the East to the West Coast cities. One day, he had told her, his squadron was given orders to take out a convoy of old school buses running through his territory. On his monitors it was obvious that there were children on those buses, many his age and younger. He refused the order, and when the guy in the seat next to him took over his station, he walked out of that room and never went back.

Instead, he defected. He turned himself over to Kreskin the Fixer, head of the biggest viajero clan on the East Coast, and from there he provided security intelligence and interface reconnaissance, and every once in a while he laundered a little dark money to keep them all fed.

When he wanted out, Kreskin got him a new identity and he wound up in the Manhattan Outzone. Kitty found him getting beat up in a bar after trying to move some cryptodollars, and as bloody and bruised as he was, he still looked cute enough for her to intervene and kick the crap out of his attackers. He hired her on the spot, and she let him sleep in her old mom's room until he got on his feet. He's still working on that, of course. People who sleep on foam mattresses are notoriously hard to motivate. But she has realized she likes his company and that she might even miss him if he left.

Once, he told her that his dream was to live a normal life

and buy himself a piece of Happyville. The biggest problem he had was escaping his past.

Kitty only has to see the look on his face to know that the past has found him once again.

Boy finishes the coffee and crushes the cup inside a sinewy hand. "You don't think I should do this, do you?"

Kitty stands with her back to the wall by the door to the kitchen, her arms neatly folded over her gray Omni t-shirt. She bites her bottom lip.

"No," she says to him. "It makes no sense. Why not just shoot Priest or leave? Or both? If you do this once, it's like opening a wound. Kreskin's just gonna keep poking at it and it'll never heal. He knows he's got shit on you now, why should he stop?"

"But..."

"Besides," she interrupts, "As soon as you hit the interface, your signature will be out there again. You'll trip some algorithm, or you'll make a mistake and lead Madoka and whoever else straight here anyway."

"But..."

She kneels and kisses him, cups his face with her hand. "I like you, Boy Eastman. I like you a lot," she says before she lithely rises back up to her feet and leans against the doorframe. "But there are better ways to pay the rent."

She kicks herself off the wall and leaves the room, closing the door behind her.

Boy is alone in a grimy grey room with a swivel chair, a desk, and a foam mattress to sleep on. She's right. He can't just do what Kreskin wants, but he has to give him something. Something inside him claws at his stomach. An empty feeling.

A hunger.

He takes the machinery out of its bubble-plastic wrapping. It's been in storage in a blue plastic chest in Kitty's room for so long that the wrapping has stuck to the molded form of the Panasony electronics, making the job more difficult. The sense 'trodes, like sticky silver beads with microthin wires, are wrapped around the Etherdeck, a procured military item in cold satin black, designated Ares IV.

The Ares IV has a stream of wires that plug into the input port of his stolen, unlicensed Deus computer. Built in Poland, its bright red plastic casing and molded keyboard with old chunky keys is kitschy and deliberately retro, designed for the billy market. Boy is no billy, he's too dragon, but he likes things in strange colors.

The whole setup has been updated for ultra-high speed bias by Laughing Simon back when he first arrived, in case he ever needed to use it again. Laughing Simon is one of Kitty's friends and a great engineer. When he fires the two machines on, they boot up instantly, faster than anything factory-made. Good. Boy's gonna need all the speed he can get.

He jacks it into the socket that runs a line into the building's sat dish. He smears a little conductive gel across his forehead, sticks the trodes to it, and taps his fingers on his knees. Green tell-tale lights glisten in the darkness of his room. The screen on the Deus computer waits for his first order. Everything's ready except Boy.

He sits cross-legged in front of the setup and hesitates. The hunger inside his guts claws him again, and he nearly buckles with tension. With his left hand, he fingers the keyboard of the Deus computer, preparing himself for sensory takeover.

With the other poised over the Ares IV, he touches the Start switch.

Just as Boy had taught the Dagger and Man Friday, so a girl called Cage introduced him to the interface on a cold London night in a Panasony-owned flat in the Camden Secure Zone.

He was twelve years old and Cage was a small, thin-boned, pretty little Bangladeshi girl with nothing better to do than follow the latest fads.

She had spent most of the day playing with her father's electronic toys. His Panasony computer... black and sleek and totally unlike the low-tech kit-boxes that Boy had seen in Pancras Wells. His wallscreen TV was always tuned into Heartland Kidz running the same tired adventures of baby-faced anthropomorphic soldiers in space jungles, fighting the evil insectoids with their nuclear battlesuits. They fought the tedium by playing the exact same characters in video games, but Cage was better than he was at those.

One day, when they raided the closet for fancy costumes, Cage came across a thin brown plastic box that she had seen her father use once. It barely weighed anything, and sat in the palm of Boy's hand, about the size and shape of a whiskey flask.

He remembers her words now, how she tried to explain the concept behind this new gizmo to this bright, but uneducated, boy, lying on the luxurious carpet of her bedroom. She tapped the ridge on her black leather swivel chair.

"See this chair?" she said. Twelve-year-old Boy Eastman nodded softly. "This chair doesn't really exist. It's just an amassment of atomic particles. But the way the light reflects from them, and the way our eyes see that light, leads our brains to conclude that this pack of particles is a chair. Without a way of translating the fact to us, it doesn't really exist. Without sight, it has no color. Without touch, it has no texture. Without taste, it's not organic. Without sound, it doesn't squeak when you turn it. Without smell, it isn't leather. A person without senses has no world. It just doesn't exist, there's no way of translating it to them."

Cage moved around the room like some eccentric

Heartland Education Channel science instructor and ended up grinning, pointing to her red telephone.

"Ever listened to the sound a modem makes when you send it down a phone line?" She made a weird screeching sound and an equally appalling face and Boy gave a little giggle.

"Data. Raw data. A computer talking to another computer. Not to us, because it doesn't speak our language, but that's by-the-by. The fact is that data has a sound. And if it has a sound, it has a smell. And a taste, and a texture and you must be able to see it. It exists. Only normally, there's no way to translate it to us."

She edged over to Boy and kissed him softly, running thin brown fingers through his spiky black hair. "Some days I go there... to this other world. Father calls it the Ether. Like ethereal, I suppose. But it's more like a chessboard than anything else. You want to go? I'll get Father to bring home another set of trodes. After that, we'll do it together..."

The processor is an empty blue cathedral. Code embodies him as the virus runs its course. There is a soft dent in the defense shell and Madoka's watchdog program lays in wait. Boy knows this, though, and avoids the obvious weakness in favor of the silent meltdown.

Another key is tapped and a silver thread streams from the melting roof where Boy has lived all this time toward the bounty. The defenses have been breached, the virus has become part of the defense program, shaping itself to the contours and Boy knows his trojan software can work well enough without him, that he can switch off any time and let a demon do the work for him. But it seems too easy, and something must be wrong.

He stays with it, observing... watching the trojan open and close files with lightning speed, knowing its true target, but running a trick that it is a routine file check. As soon as it finds the folder, the thread snaps back, and Boy sends a program to cover its tracks. It doesn't matter. The breaching virus is old and faulty and has caused a cancer in the defense shell that the watchdog can't fail to notice. Now it's bleeding data towards him, the flight plans, drone pilot roster details, drone control codes…

Boy waits just long enough for the thread to return before he tries to rescue the virus which has gone wild. The interface is slowing, his maneuvers becoming sluggish and constricted. He's reeling himself back with the data he's downloading, and trying to shut all the doors he had set up between Manhattan and Madoka, but he's too slow. Before he can tear the trodes from his forehead, he feels the crushing smash of the Madoka trace program as it finds his home shell. His senses are dazed, rocked back and forth and he is pulled like spaghetti as he sees the trace's toothy smile.

He tears the trodes from his forehead and fights for breath. Suddenly nauseated, he crawls so fast through the door but vomits across the kitchen floor before he can reach the sink. Passing out, he can sense the far-off rank smell of stagnant water and the cruel touch of a rough cloth. The stern tones of Kitty's voice echoing through his head…

CHAPTER THREE

"It's not the size of the dog in the fight, it's the caliber of the bullet in the chamber." — Big Pierrot.

Snakestrike. The pretty, dark-haired girl brings his tequila over to him and then motions him closer to her. Her voice is an urgent whisper. "Your name's Boy, isn't it?"

Boy nods.

"Man in that booth behind you was asking for you not two minutes ago. He said he was an old friend. I told him you weren't here. He said he'd wait. If you're in trouble, ace, call for another drink. I'll bring the shotgun, escort him out for you."

Boy sits back.

"When I send you flowers, what name do I ask them to put on the card?"

She laughs. She's never heard that one before. "Jess," she says.

"*Xiexie*, Jess. I owe you." He taps the bar and takes a breath before pushing himself off the stool and looking across the booths for this Mister Dangerous. He spots him immediately and knows his name is Turk.

"The fuck are you doing here, Turk?"

Turk has his arms spread along the back of the seat, a dumb, superior grin on his wide hillbilly face. He wears the same blue overalls Boy used to wear when Turk was his console neighbor at Madoka Farms. When Boy walked away from his desk that day in disgust at his orders, it was Turk who took over his position and finished the job. Boy checks Turk's belt with a glance, his holster is empty. Despite his business, he must have been forced to check it at the door.

"Thought I'd find you here, Eastman," he drawls drunkenly. "I was gonna ask you that question myself. How the hell can you live in this dump, anyways? What do the Sammies call it? Shit-what?"

"Shi Zhongxin. It's Chinese for downtown. *Luo suo*, Turk, just tell me what you want."

Turk laughs raucously, bobbing his head, gum smacking around his back teeth. "Jeez, Eastman. You been here so long, you even spoutin' like a Sammie. By the way, your friend Priest is dead. I did him myself, but not before I managed to spill your deal outta him. So gimme my flight plans and we'll be friends again."

"We were never friends. What makes you think I've got them with me?"

Turk leans forward and takes a sip from his beer, then returns to his reclining position, absent-mindedly tapping his fingers against the ultra-suede. "Because you're here see to see Mr. Priest, and Mr. Priest is not altogether here. Matter of fact, he's not all together at all, but in about five dumpsters between here and the Canal Street wall. So, because I'm not gonna repeat myself a third time, gimme my fuckin' flight plans."

Boy stares at the man's narrow eyes and sighs. There's

nothing he can do here, and he knows it. He's been in too many bar fights in backwater roadhouses with this guy to know Turk's faster and better at it than he is. Even though neither of them has had the surgery to wire up their nervous systems and make their reflexes faster, Boy just lacks the physical advantage. Hell, even with the support of Jess and some of the other Team Huawei players, he could kill the bastard and it wouldn't matter. Madoka would only send someone else even better, faster, stronger.

Leaning back he runs his hands through his spiky black hair and then takes the silver kerndrive from his jacket pocket and tosses it over to him.

"Sammie for downtown," Turk mutters. "Down is the operative word, Eastman." He turns his head to the end of the booth, which backs onto the mezzanine balcony. "Can't you play some Neil Young or somethin'? All this Sammie noise sounds the same and half of it ain't got no words!" He comes back and laughs. "You got insurance, Eastman? I'd take some out if I were you." He stands and guzzles his beer.

"And don't let those Sammies take you in. Remember Pearl Harbor. Catch you 'round." Turk slips out of the booth and past the cocktail bar, shaking his head and laughing to himself when Jess throws him a dirty look.

"Pearl Harbor? That was the Japanese! How about you read a fucking book someday!" Boy calls after his shadow.

Jess steps over with his forgotten tequila. "You okay?"

Boy takes a sip from the glass. "Yeah. Someone I hate just killed someone I don't know and now someone I actually like is going to kill me."

"I brought the rest in case you need it." She places the tequila bottle on the table.

Boy laughs and shakes his head. "No, that's fine. I need to think about how to get back at that bastard."

"Well, you know what Big Pierrot would say." She sneaks

a glass from her pocket and pours herself a tequila from the bottle.

He sighs. Big Pierrot, still the most popular show in the world after 6 years, and somehow he hasn't seen a single episode. "No," Boy says. "What would Big Pierrot say?"

"Limb removal is the best revenge."

"That's the worst advice I've ever heard, Jess."

"It's definitely not the worst I've ever given." She smiles. "My shift ends at 4 if you're still around."

He smiles and blushes a little. "I'm sort of with someone."

She nods. "Kitty? I wasn't sure if... You know. People usually hire her to protect them."

He takes another sip of the tequila. "It's complicated."

"No big deal." She picks up the bottle. "If you want another, you know where to find me. And don't forget the flowers next time?"

"Plastic ones okay?"

She nods, a wry grin on her face as she heads back to the cocktail bar. "Lilies!"

He stares into the glass. A guy got killed for that stupid run. Maybe if he had waited, he could have cased it properly and had Laughing Simon work with him on setting up a better rig, a more targeted virus. Instead, it caused a data leak and set off the alarms. He smacked his head back against the booth seat. Stupid!

The worst part is that he is still on the hook with Kreskin to provide those flight plans. Even though Madoka knows where he is, Kreskin will send guys for him, too. He would have to go back in there and find the new flight plans and it won't be anywhere near as easy a second time. He won't have a chance to get back at Turk or Madoka or anyone unless...

He brings the empty glass over to the bar and hands it to her. "You said 'limb removal', right?"

She nods. "It's the best revenge."

"Not such bad advice, after all, Jess. See you around." He heads through the door and lets the darkness claim him.

CHAPTER FOUR

"Throw me to the wolves and I will return leading the pack." — Big Pierrot.

"Nixon! How are you?"

Nixon's long, red face fills the videophone screen, all thick lips and squinty eyes. "Every day I breathe, Eastman is a good day. Are you still with that shit-for-brains Kreskin?" He has a strange voice, as if he learned how to speak from an actor in one of those ancient monochrome films; Edward G. Robinson, perhaps, or Jimmy Cagney. It's all staccato and lives only in the mid-range of the audio spectrum.

"No, not anymore, I'm a free man now." He lies.

"Word is you moved to the big city." How does everyone know where he is?

"Yes. I'm in Shi Zhongxin, I have a contract with Team Huawei." And why would he tell Nixon? What the fuck is he thinking?

"Team Huawei? That's a good tag team." Seventeenth in the league.

"Fifty-five points last night, you get a share?"

21

"My tag betting days are over, Eastman. But you didn't call me to discuss tag, or at least I hope not."

"No, Mr. Nixon. I've got something you might like. I did a run for Kreskin two days ago, Madoka drone patterns along the North Route."

"Whatever Kreskin's paying for them, I can double that." Boy knows he *could*, but would he?

"Too late on that one. Madoka wised, so they'll have changed the patterns already. But! There's something else I saw while I was there that is even better."

"Tell me."

Boy pauses. As soon as he says these next two words his life as he knows it is over. Completely upside down. There'll be no knowing what the fallout will be.

But it'll be a hell of a ride if he can pull this off.

"Access codes," he says. "Access codes for every Madoka drone operating in North America. You'll be able to control any drone in your path, send it away, crash it into a tree, or simply switch it off. Madoka will replace them, eventually. But it will take time, maybe even a whole year."

"Is this exclusive?" Hell, no.

"I'll be making only three copies, one for you, one for Kreskin, and the third will be at an undisclosed location. If I hear that either you or Kreskin have decided to shut the other out, I'll make the third public and everyone will have them. Of course, I'd rather not do that, the other viajero bosses are dicks and I don't know why anyone would ride with them."

"On that much, I can agree. Count me in. Price?"

"An even 200k in cryptomarks. I have a silo account you can drop them into - World Bank. I'll fax you the details."

"Fax?"

"More difficult to intercept." Not impossible, though. Nothing ever is.

"Pick-up point?"

"On the fax. You'll get it later today, as soon as I've got the goods."

"It's a deal, Eastman. I know now why Kreskin spoke so highly of you."

The screen turns gray.

"Who was that?" asks Kitty. She's standing half-in, half-out of the doorway to the kitchen. There is still a trace of vomit smell in the air in there from the other night.

"Nixon. Another viajero boss." He wipes sleep from his eyes and pulls at itchy hair.

"I can't believe you're planning to go back in there. They already killed one guy, and you know you're next. I can't protect you, Boy. You can't afford me."

"After this, I can. I mean… Shit, Kitty!" He moves to the door. "I'll have enough to get out of this shit-hole. And I'd really like you to come with me."

"Where?"

"North."

She glares at him. There's nothing up north but ice and gas mines. Behind her the microwave beeps. She opens the door and pulls out a steaming cup of ration coffee.

"This is a shit plan, Boy. There's no way it'll work." Kitty takes a sip and burns her tongue.

Boy goes back into his room, looking out through his window at the crumbling block across East 10th Street. Lines of age wrinkle the building. The circular port-hole windows, like a thousand eyes all cry at once.

"It bloody well better work," he finally replies.

After sending a message out to Kreskin, he checked a few old social nodes to see if anyone was looking for anything like this in case Kreskin decided he didn't like him anymore. A private military contract company called Harlequin expressed an interest in anything Madoka drone-related. Something to do with a hit they have to make on the company, the message claimed.

Boy meets them at dusk in Tompkins Square, when the day is hottest, and the shadows are longest. They exit an armored truck and Boy starts laughing. The Harlequin agent's name is Fly, a frail twig of a man who needs a metal walking stick to stand upright. Fly's known in the Outzone as a good fence, Boy used to sell stolen kerndrives to him when he was desperate for money. This is... Unexpected.

"Fly McFee, it is interesting to see you," Boy says.

McFee laughs. "Yeah, I can imagine I'd be the last guy you'd expect to be running this operation."

The boys surrounding him are typical San Angeles ronin, both six feet two inches with deep tans, dressed in loose-fitting green cargos and hooded sweatshirts, with shiny chrome eyes and the straps of their assault rifles wrapped around artificial arms. Boy has seen a million like these two muscleboys, and he's more confused than impressed.

"So..."

"The blond one is Mavik and the other one's called J.D. I won them in a poker game."

"A poker game?"

"Yeah. I won the title to a PMC company. I'm a legitimate businessman now, can you believe that? I have an office and everything."

Boy shakes his head, the smile refusing to leave. His muscleboys - or contractors, Boy realizes - don't seem to find the humor and instead fan out to watch the surrounding windows and passing traffic.

"So what's business like for you now, Boy?" Fly speaks in a dreamy, whispering tone, a voice much older than he is; looking at him with eyes that are much wiser than the frail man could ever be.

"To tell the truth, kerndrives are becoming obsolete, and I'm a really shit pony. I can't sell candy to a kid. I need to move on again."

"You should expand! Expansion's always a good thing, Boy. What was that President's catchphrase? 'If you're going to think at all, think big.'"

Fly breaks into a hoarse laugh and Boy joins in. J.D. and Mavik look calmly at the decrepit housing blocks that surround the concrete plaza of Tompkin's Square. Thermographic Panasony vision scanning the windows for threats. They have rewired nerves for inhuman speed and could probably take out a potential assassin before the hammer fell on his gun. That stuff like that doesn't come cheap, either. Most of Team Huawei who have rewired nerves had to go as far as the Tokyo Metroplex to find a neurosurgeon good enough to do it. These boys have it as standard with all the corporate and military trickery behind it. They probably don't even know about the glitches in the triggering software that runs the nervous system.

"Where's Man Friday? How's he doing these days? I haven't heard from him in a long time."

Fly pulls a vape stick from his black denim jacket and sucks on it. "He's still trying to find out what happened in Rio. Did he leave a girl behind there or something?"

Boy nods. "A wife, from what I remember."

Fly's thin eyebrows rise, wrinkling his high forehead. "Ah, makes sense now," he says. "Well, we think the Federales caught up with her and she's gone missing. He's organizing an expedition to find her, I think. After this Madoka run, we're gonna go in with him. He wishes you were running interface again. Says it ain't so much fun with you not around."

Boy slips a piece of paper into Fly's sinewy hand. The fence opens it quickly, reads it, and then sets fire to it with an old butane lighter.

"This is a big payday, Boy. Are you sure that's what you want for it?"

"Once this is over, I'm done with all of this and I'm out of here. I'm tired of running, Fly. I need a home."

"Wife? Dog? Picket fence?"

"No! That shit's for the rich." He paused and grinned. "Okay, maybe the picket fence."

Kitty watches Boy from a velotaxi waiting across Avenue B. She can see his life here burning out slowly. She can see from his blue-eyed, thousand-yard stare that his feet are getting itchy again. His track record has proven that he doesn't stay in one place for too long. She wants him here, or at least with her. The two of them aren't in love, not exactly, but what they have is more than a friendship, it's some kind of closeness that she's grown accustomed to, and now she can't afford to live without it.

As soon as this job is over, assuming he survives it, she knows he's going to have to run. And even though there's really nothing here now holding her back, she still doesn't yet know if she can go with him.

He flicks the stop switch. Sweat pours from his face, stings his eyes, and leaves salt on his pink lips. His black hair is stuck to his wet head. He gasps for air and finds the atmosphere is too thin for him in this grimy little room. He pulls the trodes from his head, rushes to the round port-hole window, and wrenches it open.

Lukewarm air hits his face and cools him down. He sticks his head out into the night's rain. It rains every night in Manhattan. Something to do with the high humidity during the day condensing when the hot sun goes down.

Across East 10th Street, three Huawei Tag Teamsters in their canary yellow jackets and purple tiger-striped skintight jeans suck on nicotine sticks and slap with each other about previous clashes. One of them breaks into a spurt of superhuman martial arts to demonstrate his actions. Just visible behind the kid's ear a biochip shines from his neural software port. Chipped for Hapkune-Do, reflexes rewired and boosted by 10 percent, zen flowing from their new Panasony eyes. Boy looks at these kids and sees the future of the world. Their future.

He slides back inside and closes the window. Walking over to the middle of the floor, he looks at the green screen of the unlicensed Deus computer and sees the results of this day's work. Two tickets to Heathrow waiting for him whenever he wants. One way. His life here is falling to pieces, and it's getting near the time to skin out. Tiny words glowing green in a dark room. He looks at that screen and knows he can see his future.

CHAPTER FIVE

"Whatever doesn't kill me had better start running." — Big Pierrot.

"Kreskin says he'll meet you outside the old Slammer Cyberena at noon."

"Times Square."

That's where he is now. The north end, across from the entrance to the Cyberena. He sits in the uncomfortable seat of a magnesium alloy velotaxi that belongs to a young Irish-American kid called Bobby, who wears a white 'BIG PIERROT SAYS WATCH YOUR BACK' T-shirt and a conical straw hat to keep the blazing sun off him. Kitty's next to him, watching the windows behind the dead neon signs. She's not happy about this choice of venue at all. It's out of Shi Zhongxin. Out of the protection of Team Huawei. Team Tencentury runs things here, and they don't like encroachment from other companies.

Boy figures the poor security of the area will work to the advantage of everyone, but he knows that Kitty doesn't get nervous without good reason. So when Kreskin's red velotaxi

28

arrives and Kitty hands him a Fuke pistol, he doesn't give it back. Boy knows his way around a gun but refuses to own one. He snaps a magazine in and loads a round, letting the hammer down softly. Before climbing out, he stuffs the thing down the back of his baggy red jeans.

Kreskin climbs out wearing a cheap business suit, hiding his eyes behind a pair of Mitsubishi anti-laser glare glasses. He keeps two of his viajero muscleboys close to him, who watch the area while toying playfully with Columbian assault rifles.

For a moment it almost looks like Kreskin doesn't recognize Boy as he strides across the street. But soon he's there and Anatoly's famous smile splits his chubby face. The huge arms extend and the two old friends hug each other with subtle reservation.

"I almost didn't want this, Eastman." Kreskin's eyes are open wide, as they usually are when he's trying to impart some kind of wisdom. "When I heard you gave this to Nixon, too, it upset me greatly. I almost put a notice out on you."

"How do I know you didn't?"

"You don't, and you never will."

Somehow, Boy doesn't feel reassured. "Well, this isn't about you and Nixon, it's about me and Madoka. They got in the way of my business, so I'm giving you the chance to get in the way of theirs."

Kreskin's smile falters. "When they find out you did this, they're going to send everyone after you. Your name's going to be mud, your face is going to be on screens everywhere. Are you prepared for that?"

Boy shakes his head. "Is anybody ever?" He hands Kreskin the kerndrive. "I'm sorry about Priest."

Kreskin smirks. "He was a cock. He thought he knew how to handle himself. I should have sent someone better. Thank you for this. This will make lives easier."

As well as death. The viajeros have few ethics when it comes to what jobs they take.

There's a stifled cracking noise behind them, a cry, and then Kitty's urgent yell: "Boy!"

He spins to see the scene, pulls the Fuke from his jeans.

Bobby's in a growing pool of blood at the edge of the sidewalk, away from the protection of his velotaxi, his life evaporating under the heat of the sun. Turk has Kitty by the throat, using her as human body armor; the cliched hostage position, with a thick chrome revolver pressed into her temple.

"Hi there, Eastman!" Turk breaks into his dumb grin showing bright white teeth and a piece of strawberry gum. "Think I'd leave here without takin' you wi' me? I think not."

Boy levels the automatic at Turk's head. Behind him, he can feel the presence of Kreskin and his goons, those assault rifle laser sights now pointing in his direction, sending shivers along his neck. Sweat drips from his chin. Not only does he have Turk to deal with, but now Kreskin's decided to take him out while he has the advantage. He has little time to think.

"Let her go, Turk!" Boy yells. "This is you and me here."

Turk whistles and makes a face. "You been watchin' too much Big Pierrot, Eastman. Come up wi' an ole cliche like that. You put away your piece an' maybe, jus' maybe, I might let your li'l lady go."

Boy shakes his head, his stomach tightening. His pistol pointing at Turk's face, but if he's off just a millimeter here, it'll be Kitty's face he'll be shooting. "Come on, man. I throw this away and I'm giving you all the edge."

Turk flicks back the hammer on the revolver, Kitty sucks in a breath. "What edge, fool! Don't try an' pull that mental shit on me, Eastman. I know you ain't gonna shoot me."

"Nothing can happen without you dying at the end of it,"

Boy says. "You run and I'll shoot you. You shoot me and I'll shoot you. You point the gun at me and I'll shoot you. You kill her and I'll shoot you. They shoot me and the two snipers I have up on the rooftops will shoot you. No win situation."

Boy cocks an eyebrow at Turk's expression. The smile falling from the fat hillbilly's face, turning into a sneer.

"You ain't got no snipers on the-"

Three high-velocity .50 caliber rounds smash into the back of Bobby's velotaxi. The right wheel collapses. Turk spins Kitty a little to the side to give himself cover from that position, but it's leaving him almost fully side-on to Boy, who's still aiming at him.

"What's up, Turk? Run out of choices? Then put your gun down."

Turk licks salt from his lips.

"Better do as he says, man. You won't be quite so good-looking with a hole in your face." Kitty's mind is racing. She's wired, but surely not as fast as any of these guys. She has to assume they're all faster than she is and Boy, she knows, has none of these advantages. Even the tiniest reflex boost is enough of an edge against an unmodified man. No, she can't outrun them, so she has to outthink them. Be faster by pre-empting them all.

"Shut up, bitch!"

"What's it going to be, Turk, eh?" Kitty can feel her wired nervous system, courtesy of Team Huawei, speeding up. The effect is like pins and needles all over her body. Once it kicks in, there's a slight vertigo and then the neural processor that runs it all from the base of her spine ramps up and the world turns slow-mo.

Frame by frame, a second of violence.

Kitty moves first. Her elbow lifts up and back to push Turk's arm away and the revolver slips from his grasp and Kitty is in the air, diving for the cover of the velotaxi. Turk is a standing target, but Boy doesn't fire at him, instead, he drops to the floor and shoots at the red velotaxi, emptying half a magazine into Kreskin.

Kreskin's goons are too slow, only now starting to speed up. Their first bursts of fire are at the place where Boy was, and find only Turk's fat body on the far side of the street, catching him in the throat and upper torso. Bullets rip through his spine and out the other side and stands motionless for a moment before he loses balance and steps backward awkwardly before he slaps against a metal shop front and slides silently to the ground in a bloody, crumpled heap of flesh.

J.D. And Mavik, the Harlequins on the rooftop of the Cyberena, are picking off Kreskin's boys with ease, pounding bloody holes through their sorry excuses for combat armor.

One of Kreskin's goons manages to follow Boy's trajectory, and when he rolls up onto his knees to fire the other half of the magazine, bullets smash into Boy's right arm and send him spinning back to the floor.

Then the kid that shot him has an instant to realize that his boss is dead before his head shatters sending blood and brain matter across the red velotaxi. This leaves one more Kreskin boy kneeling behind the red velotaxi as the cracks of gunfire echo around the surrounding buildings. Kitty stands above him with Turk's revolver in her small hands, trained at his head. He drops his rifle. Kitty walks over and kicks it away, then delivers two shots into each of his kneecaps to keep him from leaving.

Boy is screaming in agony. He's been shot before, but that was just a flesh wound. He thinks a bone's been hit here and it's drawing his entire mind to it. By the time Kitty runs over to help him, he's passed out from the pain.

Boy climbs lazily out of the cot and moves to the window. Looking out, the hot sun is going down on East 10th Street and some kids are playing soccer with a ball made from rubber bands. These kids are going to grow up tough, he thinks to himself. Street Darwinism. But there's no future for them if they can't think, and Boy knows that being smart can just beat being tough as long as you're smart enough to surround yourself with tough people. He knows cause it's not him lying in the street in Times Square waiting for Team Tencentury to pick him up. That's Turk, and Turk was tough; but stupid.

Kitty stands at the door, the one place in his room where she feels comfortable. "So, that's it, right? You're headed back to Thames Midland."

"No. Turk said I may need an insurance policy. I'm going to keep the tickets open for that."

"What about for now?"

He turns around and sees her there. He smiles. His bandaged arm doesn't hurt much anymore. Not after Kitty pressed about 320 milligrams of generic endorphins into the bloody skin. He's as happy as a rat in a hole. But he knows he really needs Kitty.

Boy shakes his head. "I want you to come with me. We've got enough money to make a new start. We don't have to go north. Fly and the Harlequins are doing a job in Rio, we could head down with them."

"Every time you touch that machine, Boy, you have to run. You do realize that, right?" Kitty seems to raise her whole face, an expression which means to Boy that she knows the answer already.

"Man Friday said he misses me."

Kitty's expression turns into a rueful grin. She shakes her head and gives him a knowing look as she edges out the door.

"Wait," he says.

She stops.

His eyes plead to her. "We don't have to stay with them. Once we get to Rio, we can go to Buenos Aires or Montevideo or... I don't know, just get a farm somewhere."

"Buy a piece of Happyville?"

He smiles. "I'm already there."

It hits her like a gut punch. "You need to heal up first. Huawei's docs are good, but not travel-the-world-two-days-after-being-shot good. Then we'll see about running away, okay?"

Boy can feel his body heating up and relaxing, like slipping slowly into a perfectly warm bathtub. Everything begins to float and tingle, except his eyelids, which stay closed for longer with every tiny blink. "Okay," he says. "Everything's going to be okay."

He doesn't see her close the door. He doesn't hear her pack her belongings into a battered old plastic duffel bag. He doesn't know that she's crying as she fumbles for her slug to call a velotaxi.

And neither of them has a clue about the two company contractors coming up the stairs to their door.

PART TWO
MONKEYTRICK

CHAPTER SIX

"Everyone wants to be a diamond, but no one wants to get cut." - Big Pierrot

Shi Zhongxin. The Manhattan Outzone. The Year of the Rat.

Boy Eastman awakes to darkness at first, then sees the red glow of his slug blinking by the wall and remembers he had finally been allowed to stay in her room that night. Groggy, he moves to wipe the blur from his eyes but feels a hand push hard down on his shoulder from behind him. He spins in the bed.

"Shush!" Kitty's eyes are wide, staring directly into his. "I heard something," she whispers before easing herself out of the covers.

She grabs a pair of jeans and slides them on, making deliberate, silent movements. There's a loaded Fuke pistol in the drawer of the bedside cabinet, but the drawer's mechanism squeaks so loud she may as well yell through a bullhorn. She throws on a sleeveless top and slides her arm under the bed, coming out with a black-bladed ceramic combat knife. She places herself at knee level beside the pocket door and motions to Boy to roll softly out of the bed and stay behind it, out of sight.

Boy complies without question.

They wait.

The handle turns.

The pocket door slides towards her. The outline of some kind of bullpup carbine rifle appears, followed by a shadow moving in a crouched position. She lets the shadow make it all the way inside before she softly slides the door closed and rams the knife into a soft area between its helmet and neck protection. Hot blood runs over her hand as she tugs at the blade's handle but the serrated back is stuck on something. The shadow stiffens and gurgles. She lets the knife go and grabs the back of its combat armor as it relaxes falling away from her. She holds on, smoothing the landing.

She pries the carbine from the dead man's fingers, then feels around his armor for a backup pistol. She finds it and silently lays it at Boy's feet. She raises two fingers to tell him to stay, then she snorts in the air five times, the action which triggers her wired reflexes. As her body tenses up, her face in the dim red glow looks so strange, so animalistic, her features jittering and her mouth so taught that he hardly recognizes her.

Then she reaches a kind of equilibrium, where her muscles become perfectly in line with the speed of her brain and she becomes serene and still. Kitty smiles at him then and blows him a kiss.

And she's stand-door-gone before he can catch it.

With no real idea how many more might be in her tiny two-room apartment, she checks first in her mother's old room, now home to Boy's cot and a mess of kludged tech and kerndrives and clothes, and it's goon-free. She steps back into the hallway with her finger on the trigger of a flashlight. As she reaches the doorway to the kitchenette, a figure appears at the end of the hallway, with a similar outline to the man she had just killed. She flicks the flashlight full beam right at the figure's face, dazzling his night vision goggles for a split second. Enough time to fire a three-round burst into the goon's chest and face and slip into the kitchenette.

Inside, she quickly grabs another knife from a cutting board and then spins back to cover the hallway. In the flash of light, her suspicions are confirmed. These aren't street goons or Tag Team players from uptown, these guys are black-uniformed, tactically equipped, and armed for bear. This is a Madoka hit squad coming after Boy for giving away their drone control codes. She knew they'd come for him, which is why they were supposed to be leaving for Buenos Aires in five hours. She just didn't realize they'd be so... Prompt.

Hell opens up at the end of the hallway. Four or more carbines start spitting rounds at her, picking chunks of plastic out of the wall next to her head, forcing her behind the kitchenette wall. She can't stay here. Not even for an instant. She has to get Boy out of the window, even if there are more out there. She and Boy are cornered here.

She pulls a kitchen stool over and stands on it, right next to the open doorway, then reaches the carbine around the top corner and fires blindly from there. It gives her a tiny window, as they direct their fire to the higher position. She kicks the stool away from under her, leaps into the hallway toward the door to her room, rolling, firing madly behind her, landing on the dead soldier inside with a sharp exhale as another gunshot rings out and another bullet whizzes past her, but from *inside*. She stares at Boy, pointing the pistol at her head. He damn near killed her coming in. She allows a cursory glance of admonition before she pulls at the squeaky drawer and takes out the Fuke and starts blasting hollow-point safety rounds filled with number 6 bird shot down the corridor. She knows she can't penetrate their ballistic armor with them, but hopes they'll hit hard enough to knock them down for a couple of seconds while she figures out how to get out of this shit.

"Check out the window, Boy. You see any friends?" she yells.

Boy flips up a blind.

She reloads the Fuke and lets loose another clip of safety rounds at the soldiers.

"Clear," he says.

"There's an escape chute in the closet. Know how to work it?"

He runs to the closet and takes out a steel frame filled with some kind of lightweight, tough cloth material. He had seen these on TV but had never used one before. Lots of people kept one in case of block fires, but they weren't mandatory. Few things were in the United States.

"Take this," Kitty swaps the chute for the carbine and heads for the window.

Boy takes position at the rapidly disintegrating doorframe and starts firing more three-round bursts at whoever the hell was there.

Kitty kicks out the window. Hot air blasts her face, but she doesn't have time for that shit. She locks the steel chute frame to the interior of the window frame and pushes out the interior material. Outside the building, gravity takes over, pulling the coated fireproof material down to the street. Or so she hopes anyway.

She taps Boy on the shoulder and takes the carbine from him. "Time to go," she says, and she kisses him hard, but so briefly.

Boy clambers over the bed and grabs a bar at the top of the chute frame. He takes one look back to see her blasting more rounds down the hallway, then swings feet first into the twisting, descending darkness.

With Boy in the chute, and her running out of the dead

soldier's ammo, she takes a millisecond to check the situation in the hallway. One soldier is down, with another dragging him out of the killzone. Another is providing cover fire, while the fourth is attaching a rifle grenade to the barrel of his carbine.

It's over. She throws a couple more three-round bursts into the hall, hoping to catch the grenadier, but without assumption and she's up and running for the chute. She drops the carbine, swings into the tunnel, and starts the twisting descent.

Behind her, the blast wave from the grenade knocks the hastily placed escape chute locks loose, and it slides, rattling, out through the window frame. She twists one more time, the inner lining of the chute contracting and expanding as she descends, like a snake swallows its prey, and then she begins to spin, free-falling in darkness until the East 10th Street embraces her.

Boy is running but turns when he hears the chute frame smash into the window of a parked car.

The street falls into near silence, only the sound of the chute crinkling in the hot breeze. It crisscrosses the street like a dead animal. In the dim blue-white of a nearby streetlight, close to the broken car, there's something still in the chute.

There's some*one* still in the chute.

"Shit, Kitty, no." He's running over to the chute, but he's too late, he knows. It - *she* is not moving. And he slows himself as he hears heavy vehicles turning onto his block, and more PMCs making their way up the sidewalk. He lifts his hands, but he still has the pistol from the dead soldier in her bedroom tucked into the back of his jeans. He thinks about making a play for it and decides that enough blood has been spilled tonight. He crouches to get onto his knees, and suddenly rifles are cracking off bullets all over him.

He drops to the ground and rolls to the sidewalk, finds a

car to duck behind. Two contractor teams are blasting at each other from either side of East 10th Street, with him in the middle. He checks behind him to see if he can make it into the doorway of the tower he has so often looked at from his window, but the security gates are down. His only choice is to escape to one end with the pistol and hope somebody wants him alive.

As he pulls the pistol from his jeans, someone starts firing an automatic grenade launcher, spraying the entire street with flechette grenades. One goes off right in front of Boy's face and kicks him onto his back.

With his heart pounding in his ears, and blood in his eyes, his world is sucked into darkness.

A Russian voice says, "Let's take a look at his eyes, shall we?"

Sarah Faraji adjusts the straps on her surgical mask and watches as the doctor lifts open the young man's eyelids, waving a flashlight across each eye. "Anything?" she asks.

"No significant pupillary response, I'm afraid." Doctor Voronin looks up at her. "Will your catch need to see?"

Faraji looks at the young man, mostly naked and fully unconscious on a cheap gurney in a poorly lit examination room, and she considers the question. She had been assigned to extract him and put him to work immediately, but the contractors she hired royally fucked that. Along with blinding their target, they happily killed probably the only thing he might have cared about. So, while she needs him for his ghosting skills, and he certainly doesn't need eyes for that, she also needs him to be on her side or he'll simply refuse to do the job at all. She has no real leverage on him, the carrot-and-stick approach doesn't work without a stick, so she can't just treat him like a piece of meat.

"He'll need to see, but my budget is already stretching. Is there an alternative to artificial eyes?"

The doctor nods and turns to the duty nurse, says: "Put him down for an ocular transplant, check the donation lists, see if there are any spare artificials, but if not, we'll just take natural. Anything else, Ms. Faraji?"

She reaches out and touches the back of the young man's head, running her blue-gloved fingers through his greasy black hair. "If we're going to be invasive, let's chip him... Two chips, in case he finds one. And install a Neural Sensory Transfer socket, too. Etherdecks are too slow with those old 'trodes now."

"Did you get that?" Doctor Voronin asks. The nurse checks the screen on her slug and nods.

"How long until I get him?"

Doctor Voronin shrugs. "He's young, he looks pretty healthy. If I start work tonight, keep him sedated, dream loops to keep him calm, that sort of thing, he should be ready in two weeks."

"Good," she says. "I'll be coming in every Monday at 9 a.m. to check the progress, understand?"

Doctor Voronin nods.

She leaves the examination room, removes the gloves, gown, and mask, and dumps them in a bin. No project is ever as simple as the executives think it will be, she thinks as she removes her scrub cap and pulls her curly brown hair back into an efficient ponytail. She'll have to go begging to that prick Austin Shelley again for more financing, which means he'll cut some other program of hers in the future or mark down her performance grades. Corporate political bullshit, she sighs, par for the course at Vijayanta Pharmaceuticals.

She checks her appearance in a mirror. Her bronze features pop against a crisp medium-grey suit and white shirt. She knows she looks great, but she's not the one she needs to impress. She places her slug on top of a wall defibrillator and calls her boss.

His face appears on the screen, he looks disheveled and effortlessly handsome, his hair perfectly messy, his shirt open and tie-free. "Sarah! Having fun in America? I can't wait to hear your progress report."

"Shelley," she says. "We have a problem."

He finds himself sitting upright on a beach with no idea how he got there. He lifts hot white sand into his palms and lets it filter out through his fingers. Behind him, a single palm tree rustles in the salty breeze, and a small tree-covered island about a mile from the beach is the only disruption in a perfect, clear ocean view.

An early morning sun washes over his skin. It dawns on him that he truly has no frame of reference for this experience, other than what he has seen on TV. He grew up in a village made up of rusting cargo containers and traveled from there to the mid-west of America, and from there to New Atlantic City. He's never actually been on a beach before, or seen the ocean.

He stands, his knees buckling at first as the hot sand shifts around his weight. That's when he notices he's completely naked. He grabs the beach towel he was sitting on and wraps it around him, then heads toward the palm tree. Hopefully, he thinks, there's some kind of shelter from this Sun on the other side of the dune.

On the other side of the dune, however, is another beach, with another small tree-covered island about a mile into the ocean. Then he understands; hot white sands, warm waters, dunes, and palm trees. This is meant to be paradise, but in reality, it's a prison. And that's when he hears the voices.

They're faint at first. Playground chatter, far-off children squealing and calling out indistinct words and laughter. He steps out in the direction they appear to be coming from, but when he thinks he's getting closer, nearer the water of one beach or the other, the voices move and appear to be coming from behind him. He simply cannot pinpoint exactly where the voices are coming from. Finally, he parks himself under the tree and coves his legs with the towel.

"Okay," he says to no one in particular while idly sifting sand with his hand. "Someone has decided to stick me in a cheap-ass beach construct and torture me with unseen children. Who do I know would want to do that to me?"

Everyone, he concludes, though he cannot come up with any names. The construct, a virtual box that can be as big and elaborate as the programmer's imagination, must be interfering with his memory. He shuts his eyes and tries to think of one person, one name, one single face that he knows, but there is only darkness.

His eyes are pulled open. The beach is bathed in angelic white light of the purest kind. He has a vision of God.

He tries to pull the blanket over over his face so the light cannot penetrate, but it is everywhere, and then those children's voices become tangible, louder. The giggles and laughter become clearer.

"Can't you see it?" he yells. "It's everywhere! The light!"

"Can't see a light. Can you see a light?"

"What light? Has he had a revelation? Has he seen... God?"

"That's what happens when you have girls eyes. You think you see God."

"Maybe he thinks he is God!"

"All-powerful! All-knowing!"

They begin to chant, "All-powerful! All knowing!" Mocking him.

He cries out to them, "I'm not all-powerful! I know nothing! I'm just a boy!"

"All-powerful! All-knowing!"

"Stop it!"

* * *

45

The voices fade. The light fizzles and burns out. The beach is gone. Beneath him now rough ground, torn-up black top. He is in an alley, one he recognizes, but cannot quite place. He knows it's close to where he grew up, but doesn't know why he's there. As his eyes adjust to the low light, he sees a group of teenage boys leaning against a wire fence on the left side of the alley. They're crowded around a smaller silhouette. New sounds are growing in the group now. Laughter, goading, stifled yelling.

"Come on, Spence! Just do it!" Calls one croaky voice, a male but adolescent, his vocal cords barely broken.

"Naw, blood! This is bullshit! Leave her, we have to be at the Wheelhouse."

"I'll do it," says another voice ahead of him.

He crouches forward on the other side of the alley, keeping a wall behind him and the shadows in front. He can just make out the scene better now. Five teenage boys stand in a circle, one holding a younger girl in a headlock with a pistol pointed at her face. One of the boys moves away from the pack: Spence, he assumes. Another, the third boy he heard and easily the oldest and largest in the group, tugs at his belt.

The girl's eyes widen and she bites down on the wrist holding the gun. That boy screams and lets go of the pistol.   The girl throws her head back as hard as she can and crunches her skull into his nose, splitting it open, then kicks the pistol across the alley. She runs after it, but quick hands reach out and drag her back into the circle, slamming her against the fence.

"Oh, you're going to pay for that, rich girl," says the third voice. He grabs her by the neck, pulls a knife, and places the blade right by her slender throat.

"Jesus, Raz!" Spence pushes into the crowd, but Raz swings the knifepoint right in front of him, and he freezes.

"She's mine, Spence. Stay the fuck out!"

The kid with the bleeding nose staggers out of the group, looking for the pistol.

He is still watching. Still crouching in the shadows. The pistol has skidded to a stop less than a meter away from him, but he can't reach it without being seen. He knows all he needs to do is just grab it, and...

The kid sees it, wipes his bloody lip, and moves toward the gun.

He grabs it, and the other kid leaps toward him and tackles him. The two wrestle for it, and the gun goes off.

He pushes the kid's limp body off him and stands in front of the other four boys. He wants to say something cool. Something Big Pierrot on the TV would say, like "Giving a fuck doesn't go with my outfit." Or "My middle finger salutes you." But in real life, people don't hang around to listen to cool lines. There's four of them and one scared boy shaking a gun at them and they've decided to take their chances and run at him all at once.

He wants to close his eyes as he pulls the trigger on each of them, but they won't close. The face of each one - Spence's surprise, another's questioning, Raz's ineffectual anger, and the final expression of total fear - remains imprinted on his retinas.

Darkness now. The sound of crying. The lost echoes of gunshots. The wet warm smell of running blood. The pistol makes a sharp crack as he drops it to the concrete.

"You okay?" he says to the girl in the darkness.

"I've felt better. They would have killed me if you hadn't arrived, you know."

"Yeah."

"Take me home, please?" she pleads.

"Sure. Where do you live?"

"Battle Bridge."

He nods. Battle Bridge is a Panasony compound walled off from the rest of the city. "What are you doing out here?"

She looks away, ashamed. "I… I fought with my dad. I ran away from home."

He reaches out his hand. "Well, if I fought with my dad, I'm sure he'd have been worried about me at night by myself. Let's get you home."

The cold shaky touch of her hand in his. Her body set in a weak crouch. Her free hand holding her torn silk blouse together. She stands and they walk slowly back to the gates of Battle Bridge together in silence.

There aren't any children around, either he left them behind on the beach, or he shot them all in the alleyway. But in his dream, in her father's apartment, their voices still mock him like mind-ghosts, echoing in a virtual wind.

He hides from them in the dark warmth of a closet and cries. He wishes someone older was here to tell them all to shut up. He can't seem to do it himself.

A whisper from the shadows behind him. Soothing, but so unexpected and shocking that it nearly unlocks his bowels.

"Don't be afraid."

So simple. He frantically searches the wardrobe, throwing furs and leather coats and company uniforms to each side to find the voice, but it isn't there.

"Look down."

There she is, the girl from the alley. A young desi girl about twelve years old with long black hair and beautiful hazel eyes. He quickly climbs into a fur coat and wraps himself in its luxury. This is her father's apartment, he remembers. She smuggled him into the Panasony Battle Bridge compound through the same fire exit she had used to escape the other night. Her father was working in an office somewhere in the massive facility, barking orders at underlings and persuading overlords. He was rarely home these days.

She ran her fingers through his hair, fascinated by its greasiness. "You never told me your name the other night," she says.

"It's Boy."

"What a strange name."

"Actually, it's Babyboy," he doesn't know why he said that aloud, as if Babyboy were less strange than Boy. He never tells anyone his real name as he has always been teased for it. The kids, especially those in the container village by Pancras Wells, will find and exploit any weak points. "My mum couldn't think of a name. The doctors put 'Babyboy' on my temporary birth document and my mum liked it. Only she called me that. Everyone else calls me Boy."

"I like Babyboy. It's the default name, but no one chooses it, so it's even more unique." She nestles herself among a pile of ushanka hats. "So you were born 'Babyboy', now you're 'Boy'... When you reach eighteen, will you change it to 'Man'?"

Boy laughs. "No! 'Man Eastman'... It doesn't really work, does it?"

"Too many 'mans'," she says.

"Yes." Then, "What's your name?"

Pain enters his body and splits the skin envelope in a thousand places and he's crying out for mercy as he explodes, atom by atom, hooks grabbing every element of his being and pulling it apart.

Then darkness again.

Sarah Faraji is still checking her slug for messages when she enters the pastel-walled recovery ward. All the beds are full, she meets Doctor Voronin at the third bed on the right. Last week he was late, and she had made sure that wouldn't happen again.

Voronin hands her an autoscroll. She pulls the flexiscreen from the cylinder and calls up a series of charts, which display across its translucent film. "Progress report, Doctor Voronin."

"We began weaning him off the sedative two days ago. The final dose was an hour ago. We expect him to be awake and ready for some simple food around lunchtime."

"Do you still have on that dream loop?" She can't seem to find that information on the graphs.

"Yes and no. He's overwritten the beach construct we gave him and has built his own, it would seem."

Faraji looks up, surprised. "While unconscious?"

Doctor Voronin nods.

She blinks. "You gave an unconscious man a construct to occupy his brain with and he rewrote its code?"

"For the most part, he seems happier in the new one."

"For the most part," she presses.

"Yes." He decides against telling her about the seizures. They are infrequent and probably just a side effect of the construct's re-coding. If she's interested, he figures, they are mentioned on the chart, so all she has to do is-

"What are these seizures he's been having?"

"We're not sure, Ms. Faraji. We're assuming that these are caused by glitches in the code he has written in the construct. Perhaps there's an 'I' he forgot to dot, or a 'T' he never crossed."

She clicks a small button and the autoscroll pulls closed. "Have you thought about perhaps unplugging him from the construct?"

"Have you thought," Voronin snatches the autoscroll back from her, "Of how you would react if your consciousness were plugged into an artificial reality for two weeks and suddenly somebody switched the world off? With all due respect, Ms. Faraji, I have seen what that can do to a person's mind and it's not pretty at all. We have looked after your catch to the best of our abilities. As of 5 p.m. this evening, he will be discharged. Please see to it that a representative of your company is here to claim him."

She stares at the doctor. "I will be here at 4 p.m. to make sure the forms are completed and that we are not overcharged." She pulls her slug from her pocket and sets a reminder in the calendar. As she's leaving the ward she turns and says, "By the way, Doctor Voronin, I was on the research team at Brookes that wrote the book on neural interface discontinuation syndrome. I know all about the tremors, dysphoria, and dizziness. It's rare, and I highly doubt that someone who has spent so much time working with Etherdecks that they can re-code a whole fucking construct while under full sedation would have too much trouble coping with the transition, do you?"

Voronin is unable to close his mouth as the ward doors slide shut behind her.

An alarm sounds as if on cue. Eastman is having another seizure, his body squirming against the loosely-fastened restraints they have placed over his wrists and ankles. A nurse rushes in, but Voronin waves her off.

The nurse is confused. "Doctor! He needs…"

"No more sedatives, Geetha. He leaves today. He needs to be woken in 2 hours, showered, and ready for discharge by 5 p.m., understood?"

He watches the young patient as the seizure subsides and his body relaxes. He cannot wait until this kid is someone else's responsibility.

The pain is gone and he is new again. He has spent a second childhood in a Panasony flat filled with the voices of children who taunt him. But the girl, whose name has become the very embodiment of Pain, always protects him. When she's there, the other children go away. She seems to have this power, this command over them all.

"You heard the voices again, didn't you?" she asks him.

He nods solemnly. "I have to go home today."

"I'll see you again," she says.

But he's not so sure. He's scared again. "What if I don't?"

Softly, she kisses him on the mouth. Her hazel eyes bore into his. "You will. I promise."

Sheepishly, he pretends to wipe his mouth with the back of his hand, but really he savors the sensation of her kiss. "How about one more game?"

"Yes!"

Boy and Pain play games in the darkness of the closet in her father's apartment, just as they have been doing for days, weeks, perhaps. The game is always intangible, the rules always flexible, and no matter what name they give the game, Pain always wins.

Every time.

CHAPTER SEVEN

"What does hell look like? Me. It looks just like me."
--Big Pierrot

Soho. The London Red Zone. The Year of the Rat.

Years ago, before the Black November computer virus caused the markets to crash and dropped the world into an economic downward spiral of recession, food shortages, riots, and wars, people came to the inner cities of Europe to shop, go to museums, stroll in the parks and visit historic landmarks. Many companies have tried over the years since the Restoration to invest back into the inner cities with limited success. Those who did found they had to turn their facilities into fortresses to separate them from the urban poor. The higher echelons of humanity moved out of the centers like ripples in a lake, leaving rings of urban development behind in varying degrees of decay. Sometimes those rings would smash into each other creating one huge urban landscape.

In Britain, the Thames-Midland Metroplex was formed that way. Where the luxury residential blocks come crashing together, one can just make out the Eurotrans monorail stations, designed to mainline the many worthy survivors to their final destination, the last escape route, the Marseilles Aerospaceport in southern France, where the top of the heap flew up the gravity well and into the orbital stations.

Thames-Midland's middle rings consist of corporate compounds and factories. Vast gleaming spires of industry and commerce, blinking yellow, blue, and white lights across the night skies. Within the central circles lay wastelands, shanty towns, and off-grid industries left for dead by most of the regular citizens, teeming with immigrants and refugees from the high corporate culture. The Americans call places like these "outzones", the Europeans call them Red Zones, and a velotaxi just dropped Sarah Faraji and Boy Eastman off on the corner of one of the most notorious ones.

He helps her leap over a sewer run to reach a raised sidewalk, broken and weed-ridden. At the end of Tottenham Court Road, at the junction of Oxford Street, trucks and fences block the entrance to Soho, with armed militia, some no more than ten years old standing guard. He can feel them watching them both as they walk carefully up to the corner. Behind the barricade, the architecture is a mishmash of pre-Black November buildings, prefabricated building blocks stacked on top of each other, and the same kinds of shipping container units he used to live in just north of here. Atop the structures, satellite dishes and wireless aerials poke at the gunmetal sky from the crevices between solar panel arrays like weeds bursting through pavement cracks.

The velotaxi speeds away, back to the relative safety of Tottenham Court Points, they cross the street and allow themselves to be searched, pushed around some, and questioned. Eastman holds up a piece of yellowing paper with a blue X scrawled on it, and behind that about a thousand Euros in small bills. The perimeter guards allow them through with an escort of two heavily armed tweens on electric bikes, their rifles almost as large as their own skinny frames.

Sarah tries to memorize the route in case she needs to report it. The escorts take them past the barricades at Soho Street and around the vegetable garden in what was Soho Square park, down Carlisle Street, and then a sharp right at a building adorned with a large black metal sculpture of a star-covered woman with butterfly wings holding garlands of flowers and faces attached to the wall above the door. To Sarah, it's the strangest thing to find here in the middle of all this decay. She's still looking back at it when the escort stops, and she finds herself standing in front of a plain white wooden door with a blue X spray-painted on the outside just like Boy's paper scrap. The dull thump of drums and subsonic basslines leak through the door frame. The door unlocks and the escorts show them through before leaving to head back to the barricades.

Blue Cross is the main hangout for the 21 Brotherhood, the gang that controls this Red Zone. It's packed wall-to-wall with long-haired desis in leather jackets and molded Kevlar impact armor suits sprayed in a variety of bright neon colors. Boy told Sarah to dress down, so she's wearing a white lace blouse and black silk jeans and now she feels completely ridiculous.

She follows him through the dark crowd and attracts a couple of glances here and there from the men, but not enough to make her feel any smaller than she already is. Out of her depth, she needs someone like Boy to keep her afloat. The only satisfaction is knowing that without her, he'd already be dead.

Boy is pushing through this crowd looking for one person, and when he finds the young man at a table with a few friends, the poor kid can't recognize him.

The young man is dressed as a slicer, with a baseball jersey, black Big Pierrot T-shirt, leather jeans, and Kevlar-plated, knee-high boots, but his black desi hair is too short, and the chrome of the neural interface sockets in his skull behind his ear flickers in the dull orange of the candles. He fits, but he doesn't fit; a person Boy, the eternal Stranger in a Strange Land, can completely identify with.

"Long time, no see, Mo."

Motorhead is drunk as usual and strains his memory to name the face. Boy finds it impossible to believe that this seventeen-year-old has taken his place with the 21 Brotherhood.

Finally, Motorhead makes a noise. "Who the fuck are you?"

Boy's face is expressionless. "What, don't you remember the Boy? I used to run with you back in the Year of the Dog."

Motorhead returns to his drink. "Try another one, ace, the Boy's dead. The Americans got him. Blew him and his girlfriend up in Manhattan."

Some of the bigger guys at the table stand up to move him along, but Boy doesn't budge. "Seven Stars," he says. "That night in the Dog's summer when we got shitfaced? There was a woman - black hair, pure white dress - I basically bribed you to get her slug digits for me and she was a narc and damn near busted all of us."

"Look," Motorhead doesn't even bother looking up. "There were a ton of people there that night and I don't know you, and if I don't know you then you don't belong here, so…"

Boy leans right into his face. "How about when you got caught in a feedback loop inside the Credit Suisse kernel and I had to improvise a diversionary subroutine to break you out? Remember how I can't code for shit? You flatlined, Mo. Forty-five seconds. It was blind luck that Man Friday was watching our backs that day and pulled you out, or we'd both be toast. How many people did you tell about that? Hmm? Uncle Minh? Your brother?"

Now he has Motorhead's attention. No one except the Boy knows about the Credit Suisse failure. The bank's infosec team had left a honeypot neither Motorhead nor Boy could resist. It was a rookie mistake and for business. The shock of recognition hits him, a smile widens across his face.

"Jesus, Boy! You look like shit. What the fuck are you doing here? And what are you doing bringing a luxe to our town?"

Boy looks at Sarah standing behind him, a furtive gaze in her hazel eyes. She gives a hint of a shrug and hides her thumbs in the back pockets of her silk jeans. Behind them all, next to the door, a fast fistfight breaks out. Nothing special. The bouncers don't even bother to get involved.

"I'm in trouble, Mo. Real trouble."

Motorhead cocks his head to the left. "Yeah," he says. "When have you ever been out of trouble?"

Boy says they need a place to talk. Somewhere private. Motorhead picks one of the neon lions around a broken Nelson in Trafalgar Square, the one that faces north toward the foggy outline of the four huge cylinders of Tottenham Court Points that thrust into the clouds above the Red Zone.

They sit on the plinth in the lion's red glow. Motorhead takes out a small yo-yo and starts to run tricks with it.

"Where did you go? I mean, Uncle Minh went apeshit after you left. I nearly died because of you. He thought I'd tried to cut you out or something."

"I went to the U.S.," Boy says. "Got a job monitoring drones at Madoka Farms. I figured their security would keep you and all the rest off my back for a while. But... things happened there. We were running missions against the nomads who were smuggling food and drugs and anything else worth a cent between the east and west coasts. One day we got a whole convoy of trucks and buses going through my district, and I could see the buses had kids on them. You know, families. Sometimes they use them as shields to protect the cargo. I got an order to take out everything on the road, including the buses. I refused to obey that order and quit the company, but the guy in the booth next to me took my drones and did it anyway.

"So I joined the opposition, hooked in with one of these nomad groups, they call themselves viajeros. I helped drive, surfed the ether every now and then to launder finances, grey hat work, the usual stuff. Stayed about a year with them before I left for New Atlantic City - Manhattan. I met up with this smartgirl called Kitty and started selling kerndrives to Team Huawei, so I was a pony there for a while. Then I got into some mess that hooked me back to an etherdeck and now I'm here."

"What happened to Kitty? Is the luxe holding her?"

"I have a name," Sarah says.

Boy shakes his head. "She was caught in the crossfire during my extraction."

"Then why the fuck are you helping her?"

"Sarah Faraji," she continues. "Information Services Division, Vijayanta Pharmaceuticals.

He slides a small blue laminated business card across the cracked stone to Motorhead. Centered words embossed on the plastic next to a patchy videostat. 'Boy Eastman. Information Services Division. Vijayanta Pharmaceuticals IG.' The face in the videostat is subdued. Shameful. The face of someone press-ganged into the company.

Motorhead nods, then slides the card back to his old spar. "I don't get it. Why the obituary?"

Sarah steps in. "We aren't the only company who wants Boy. The night we extracted him, Madoka sent a hit squad after him and tore up his face with a grenade. We needed to make sure no one else would come looking."

"But why you?"

Boy nods to Sarah. She stares at him coldly, then eventually gives in. "Ever heard of Ghostdancer?" she asks Motorhead.

The young ghost frowns in thought. "Is that an Artificial Intelligence codename?"

Sarah nods. "Vijayanta's," she says with some pride in her voice. AIs are few and far between in the Year of the Rat. It costs a lot of money to program one. Far cheaper to get the donated braintapes of some company executives and edit them into a single Digital Intelligence. DIs are far more common, so much so that most advanced governments have one as an advisor, and many big companies keep one on the executive board. AIs, however, are corporate status symbols. An advertisement of their multinational wealth.

"So, it's your AI. So what?"

"It's gone. We've lost it."

Motorhead breaks into laughter. The sound echoes around the ancient square, a confusing collage of cruel ambiance.

Boy and Sarah aren't laughing. They each watch Motorhead in their own way: Sarah through the scared eyes of someone whose job is on the line, and Boy through eyes that once belonged to a girl. When Motorhead looks up at them, his laughter slows.

"I'm sorry. But that's pretty funny."

Boy and Sarah's serious looks give the game away. He slowly realizes exactly why they have come to see him, and the joke isn't funny anymore.

CHAPTER EIGHT

"Peace through superior mindpower." --Big Pierrot

The suite on Floor 113 at the Miramar Hotel in the center of the St. James Green Zone has a dry, air-conditioned taste to it. Motorhead finds himself pulling his stuck tongue from the roof of his mouth as he waits with Boy for Sarah to get dressed down again. Sarah doesn't have any street clothes. She's all gray company suits and maroon Vijayanta ties. More used to this kind of life, up here in the sky, where you can't even see the Red Zone beneath the dirty gray clouds that blanket the entire view from the window. Motorhead looks out at them, they look like they could take his weight if he just opened the window and stepped out.

Piercing the clouds far away are the columnar towers of various other Green Zones. Battle Bridge, Tottenham Court Points, Bowling Green, Camden, Canbury, the tip of the Smallpox Hospital spire, and the various billowing stacks of the dustzone workhouses. Underneath, he knows, are the countless crumbling, uncompleted towers of the Red Zone, none of which stand more than 30 stories high.

Unlike Motorhead, Boy has tasted rooms like this before. Nothing new, but this one has had his skin crawling since he walked through the door. He distracts himself by checking out the Disney channels on the TV. Then, realizing that they only make the feeling worse, he switches off the set.

Now utter silence.

Motorhead fidgets, his hands sliding nervously in and out of the pockets of his black and orange baseball jacket. He slumps down on the couch and runs his fingers over ultravelvet smoother than the skin on a 50 Euro joygirl. He succumbs to the urge to take off the blue pilot's cap he's wearing and spins it around on a finger. Finally, bored, he springs back to his feet.

"Have they got room service here?" he says. "I always wanted to call for room service."

Boy points him to a box in the corner. There's a long menu stuck next to it claiming to return the order within fifteen seconds. He reads the instructions: you say your order and it appears via canister in a box underneath the screen. Motorhead orders a bottle of cider.

"Want anything?" he offers to Boy. His old friend shakes his head. "Fair enough."

When the cider arrives 12.48 seconds later he opens it and drinks it all at once. A lot of flavor, no bubbles. He wonders if it's flat or that's the way luxes like it.

He stands in awe of the room, scared yet admiring. "Like the places in the TV soaps, innit, Boy? One of those luxe places Big Pierrot stays in when he's busting down a suit. Only in color."

Boy sits down with his hands in his lap and tries to think of nothing. It's impossible. That uncomfortable feeling keeps coming back, and he knows it's tied to his dream, the one he had in his coma with the children and the girl called Pain. Somewhere there is a link in all this. He had to be here for some other reason than Vijayanta's threat, but his mind is averting it; every time he tries to think about her, tries to remember her face, he thinks of something else. Remembering is the key to the pain he is feeling, but remembering what?

He looks at Motorhead, but Mo's trying to find a pocket in his jacket that will fit the bottle. Real petroleum plastic, worth a lot on the streets of the Red Zone.

No. Mo wouldn't know. He wouldn't remember.

The sun is starting to break through on this side of the Miramar building and its tiny arc pours red-purple light into the room through large circular windows. The light brings out the contours and some of the unhealable scars on Boy's face. Motorhead can see for the first time that his black hair is all implanted and bald patches show through it, which helps explain why it's longer than Boy ever used to allow. When Boy first appeared in the Blue Cross, Moorhead didn't recognize him, but the closer he looks, the more he knows that it's not just Boy's appearance he doesn't recognize. Something's horribly wrong here. Vijayanta may have put Boy's body back together, but his soul is broken. Boy has lost his old self, and it sends a stealthy shiver crawling down Motorhead's thin neck.

It takes them two hours to reach Covent Garden in the back of a velotaxi. Boy spends most of the ride watching the beggars and street vendors and turning down offers from the joyboys and joygirls trading in the darkness under the city's towers. Motorhead has decided Sarah needs a boyfriend and seems determined to find out why she doesn't have one (career, no time, little interest) and drops casual hints that he could fill the role. She takes it calmly, answering his questions, giving him just enough to seem interesting, but not enough to seem interested.

Motorhead himself talks but doesn't really listen, catching only the tiniest squalls of information in her life story. Born in

Milton Keynes, the center of Thames Midland. Followed her father into computers at Logica, a Vijayanta subsidiary. Contracted by Vijayanta and, after only three years, taken on as staff. Being the team leader of the Ghostdancer Rogue Hunt is just another step up the corporate ladder for her.

"I nearly cried when Ghostdancer disappeared," she tells him. "We looked for it everywhere within the system. But it was nowhere. No trace."

"How come we're doing it this way? I mean, you lose something that big and it's a Fed problem, no? Fednet should be doing this."

"Let's just say that Ghostdancer knows some things that we don't want to go public. Understand? Best to keep your trap shut about this." Her voice is stern but calm, yet still, her temperature bunny-hops a degree.

"So remind me one more time why I should help you and the Boy find it," he asks her with a frown.

"Do you enjoy life?" she replies.

He nods as the velotaxi pulls up to the market.

"Then you do as I tell you," she says.

Covent Garden Market is a technical bazaar. Rusting corrugated iron and sheets of gas-planet PVC shroud a maze of tiny tables, stalls, and open cases. The unfinished towers surrounding the square cast a grim shadow, and though the far-off sky is blue, twinkling with the new stars of low-orbit workstations, down here the air is thick and sweaty.

"Who did you say we could find here again?" Sarah asks.

Motorhead barges his way through the slow-moving crowds, jostling with scores of people who seem intent on just standing and looking at the merchandise, rather than buying or moving on. The ponies sell kerndrives, neural implants for those who like plugging things straight into their brains, refurbished Fednet computers, valve amps, monochrome

TVs, and even headset radios at their stalls. None seem to want to undercut the others' prices.

"Nukie. He's one of the best engineers this side of the river. He's the only guy I know who could scratch-build you a deck in the time you want. He did mine in two days."

Nukie is a pale steamer. His hair trails lank and greasy around his broad shoulders. Eyes wide open and wild, with pinprick pupils. Standing taller than anyone Sarah has ever seen, at least two meters high. Sarah concludes that Nukie is the biggest, ugliest man this side of Milton Keynes.

"Lo, Mo. Who're they?" Nukie's dialect has slowly tempered in the London Red Zone. A product of growing up in one place and having to work in another. South Shields, the small industrial complex where he was born, was abandoned by Nissan, and the whole workforce is now dotted around Thames Midland trying to find new jobs. Nukie's father worked on computer components for Nissan airmobiles. His son believes his technical flair is hereditary.

"This is Sarah. And this is Camden Town Boy. They're clean, they're with me."

"Pleased to make your acquaintance," he says to them. His face blank to Boy's old handle. The Boy must have been before his time, even though when Nukie smiles, his scarred face makes him look old enough to be their grandfather.

"So what're you after?"

Boy steps in before Motorhead can make any compromises or deals. "I need an etherdeck with military-grade signature masking, nitro-cooled, clocked at about 10 petahertz, more if you can get it. It'll need to run about five kerndrives at zero latency. And a clean Fednet computer for the software design."

The twisted smile becomes a toothy grin. "Not after much, are we? I'll have both for you by tomorrow morning if you're willing to pay for it."

"Depends on how much you're willing to charge."

Sarah tries to follow the deal as it goes down, but three slicers by the stall behind them have started a scuffle over the price of a neural implant. Just like the slicers in the Blue Cross, they wear insect-like kevlar armor suits, spray-painted in wild day-glo colors. One of them wears a jacket like Motorhead's: black and orange leather baseball-style, with a pool-ball patch on the breast bearing the number 21, for the Brotherhood.

Sarah stands back and watches everything. In a place like this, it's all she knows how to do.

"How does it work?"

"What?"

"The 21 Brotherhood. How do they keep going?"

Night in the Red Zone. Sitting in a corner of the Blue Cross, Boy and Sarah watch the slicers dance. If she didn't know better, Sarah would have thought it was a brawl. A living pincushion of flailing fists and boots. She looks away from the floor and catches a glimpse of Motorhead at the bar, joking with some of the other long-haired desis. As soon as he looks over, she turns back to Boy, who gulps down a mouthful of cheap fizzy cider.

"Uncle Minh is the bossman, right? He has contacts in most of the companies, siphons stuff from them, and gets our ponies to spread it around in the Red Zone. Just simple merchandising, really. Everything from powdered milk to neural implants. The ponies get it all for free and pay back what they sell. Some of them have stalls in the markets, some have real shops under Brotherhood protection, but a lot just go out on their slices and sell stuff on the streets. If they don't sell something, they give it back so someone else can. Anything gets lost or damaged and the pony has to pay for it."

He finishes the last of the cider from a reusable steel bottle. "It sounds complicated, but it's a pretty simple way of giving people out here what they need. The slicer gangs live or die on the merchandise they can push."

Sarah notices herself fidgeting with her hands and slides them into the pockets of a pair of black leather jeans Motorhead had loaned her. "That's not complicated, that's just multi-level marketing."

"Neither is using an etherdeck."

"I've never done that either." Looking back to the dance floor, she unwittingly catches Motorhead's attention again.

"Sounds like you had a deprived childhood."

"Yes. I suppose I did."

Sarah jumps when Motorhead slides in behind her. She didn't notice him creep around the dance floor. "You dancing?" he asks. He wraps his arms around her waist and shakes her a little.

She laughs in shock, squirming. Then escapes by grabbing the crotch of his jeans and squeezing them short and hard.

"I'll take that as a yes then," he says after a long breath. "You coming, Boy?" And she drags him away into the flailing crowd in the pit.

Boy watches them for a time, Sarah specifically. Only two days in the Red Zone and already she's sinking in. The Red Zone has claws. It grabs and sticks and never lets go. And if you do escape, it'll scar you forever. He snorts a laugh at them, picks up his bottle, and takes it to the bar for a refill.

The following morning, Boy is woken from the now-nightly Pain dream by a tickling sensation on his cheek.

Unconsciously, he shifts to scratch his face. His fingers knock an unfazed roach to the dusty carpet in front of his nose. The roach scuttles off towards the safety of the skirting board. Boy opens his other eye and remembers how

Motorhead convinced him to sleep on the floor at his place after a night at the Blue Cross.

"Drink, Boy?" Motorhead is standing at the door to the kitchen, just like Kitty used to do in Manhattan.

Boy has a dry mouth filled with carpet dust, so he answers with a nod. He feels like telling him about the dreams, but he decides to leave that in case of emergency. He doesn't want the younger ghost to know everything.

"Can I ask you something, Boy?" Sounds of Motorhead shuffling around the tiny kitchen. "How much thumb has she got on you, eh? How badly do you belong to her?"

He rubs his eyes and yawns. "Well, I can't say she saved my life, but..." A deep sigh. He sits up. "Look, if I find this thing then they might leave me alone." He almost feels like he's convinced himself.

"Must be weird, being officially dead. Means you have to really lay low."

Boy agrees to himself. Yeah. Really weird.

"That reminds me," Motorhead changes the subject. The atmosphere from the kitchen seems to lift, like elevator doors opening to let out a claustrophobe. "Heard this joke the other day. Why did the monkey fall out of the tree?"

Boy stands and pulls sleep from his girl's eyes. "No idea," he says.

"Because it was dead."

He shakes his head and gazes around the living room properly for the first time. Even for a single man, this place is too cluttered. Empty keyboards, hollow shells of bright green Fednet computers, kerndrives of Kafig-Zucht, Girls Lieben Dicke Schwarze, and other less interesting skinflicks. Holoposters of Kerry Swaine and lesser-known VirtuSense stars taped to the walls.

All shit and no shine, Boy laughs to himself. He used to have a room just like it but with perhaps a little less porn everywhere. Courtesy of Uncle Minh, the man at the top of the 21 Brotherhood.

The younger ghost finally comes back in with Federal welfare coffee. "You'd better get ready. It's nearly eight. Sarah'll be here soon, and I've got a date with Uncle Minh."

"Say 'Hi' to him for me, will you?"

Motorhead gives Boy a wary look. "You're kidding, aren't you? After what you did?"

Boy shrugs. "I don't know how long I'll be here, and I figure I'll need some friends if I want to stay alive."

Motorhead nods, understanding.

"Anyway, where to today?" Boy asks. He burns the roof of his mouth with the coffee. At last some sensation there.

Clapping rough brown hands, Motorhead replies. "Etherland, matey. Your toys have arrived."

CHAPTER NINE

"I aim to please. I shoot to kill." --Big Pierrot

"So you say he wants to patch things up?"

At first glance, one might think that Uncle Minh is made entirely out of wooden blocks. His short black hair sits in a perfect part on top of his square face, connected to a solid rectangular body with thick arms and legs hidden in a well-tailored grey suit. Even his thick glasses are square-framed so that from a distance he resembles a cute 8-bit video game character.

In reality, Uncle Minh is a monster of indescribable proportions.

Motorhead squeezes a soft squash ball. Left hand first. Then right. Then back again. Tension: release. Tension: release. Everyone knows that Uncle Minh has an evil spirit in him. One that waits for the one time when no one will expect it to take control.

Motorhead has seen the evil spirit and survived, albeit by the skin of his teeth. He has mastered a way of getting around the man by being brutally honest with him, yet another trick he learned from Boy Eastman. After Boy left for America, he took over as Uncle Minh's ghost, on call to the man whenever he needed to know things. Uncle Minh is a man who needs to know everything.

The young ghost nods and throws the squash ball at the wall of his office, situated in one of a block of densely packed containers, then catches it in the other hand.

"He says he's making a start again in London and he doesn't want any enemies."

"Is that how he really feels? I mean, I don't know, I want us to be friends again, but I can't take him on with the Brotherhood because you're here now. However, I'd rather he was on my side than with the Kistnas, or, even worse, December Flowers, you know? What do you think, Mo? Is he for real?"

Motorhead shrugs and sighs.

"Don't know," he says. "He's changed a lot, but I don't know if that's him, or something that Vijayanta did to him. He seems lost."

"He walked into my town as if he owned it and didn't come to see me first. No one is that lost."

"He was brought directly to me. Once I confirmed it was him, I made sure we went to neutral ground. There was no guarantee I was going to help him. There still isn't."

Uncle Minh shrugs. "If he's making an effort to patch it up, then I can't really say no to him. But if he tries to go against me again, I'll drop him in a meat grinder and feed him to the fucking pigs. You can quote me on that."

"Hate to say it, Uncle, but he's been killed once already. I don't think he cares what happens to him now."

Uncle Minh puts his thinking face on and Motorhead waits, bouncing the ball against the wall. He knows that the Boy is back at his place waiting for the Recon program to map out Vijayanta Core 274, Ghostdancer's home. They are both being extra careful about this affair. Neither of them has ever done this kind of job before. Rogue Hunting. Hard enough job finding something that exists. When it breaks out and could be anywhere in the world? Motorhead finds himself hiding his face behind a bony hand.

"Get him to see me. Tell him I'm prepared to forget the whole thing as long as he does. How does that sound?"

Six Brothers escort him to his flat on their slices -- fast electric bikes. Their long hair drags in the wind. This is what he joined for, Motorhead remembers, the feel of the wind on his face. Now the ether has hold of him and refuses to let go. It's a similar feeling, a powered rush through empty space, but riding a slice is a damn sight safer. Even with all the other slicer teams around.

Saying namaste to his escort, he gives the plastic fairings on his slice a quick wipe over with his jacket cuff and forces himself up thirty flights of concrete stairs in pitch darkness.

"How's it looking?" Motorhead asks.

"None too good."

Boy is slumped in a fuzzy brown armchair with a collection of pistachio shells around his feet. A fly buzzes around the shells, feeding on the detritus of half a day's studying.

"So what happened? You can tell me, I'm a doctor." Motorhead takes the jacket off and hangs it on the handle of his bedroom door. He clears a space for himself by kicking a few cider bottles to the walls of the room and sits down on a battered copy of Gothic Lolita magazine.

"Recon program mapped the core, and there's a huge hole in the node where Ghostdancer should be. Want to see?"

Motorhead switches on the Fednet computer and calls up the image. In two dimensions it most resembles the crystalline topography of an electron microscope picture. Silver edges and thin blue strands stretch across the image, and in the center a tiny neon hole in the core's edge.

"Well, you're not fucking about, it's gone. How the hell do you steal an AI?"

Boy snorts a cynical laugh. "No one stole it, Mo. Look at the shape of the hole."

Motorhead looks carefully, then fiddles with the perspective to get a better look. The hole in the core's opaque neon glow is giant and empty, but other elements are missing, a shadow within the hole that disappears in the fog of the core.

"Ghostdancer destroyed some of the system when it went," Boy says. "I called Sarah and she said that checks out. They're running a diagnostic now, and they'll make some repairs. But it all means that it wasn't stolen. See that shadow there? I've been wracking my head for hours trying to think what it could be. Unless the stories about witch-holes are true."

Motorhead shakes his head at the screen. "A witch-hole... But that would mean it burned its way out."

Boy looks closer at the screen. "Yeah. Or maybe it didn't escape outward. Maybe it escaped inward. Like how a star goes nova and then rapidly condenses and forms a black hole." He trails off. Examining the scan closer and closer, lost in his growing hypothesis. "Yeah... Like a star going nova. That would explain the shadow."

A frown of awestruck confusion pulls at Motorhead's lean face. "This isn't a star, Boy. It's an Artificial Intelligence. How the fuck does it go nova?"

Boy breaks away from the thoughts he's riding and shrugs. "Beats the shit out of me."

They drew wires and Boy lost. Now he's here, a floating decimal point in the ether. A meaningful nothing in a vast sensorium that doesn't exist.

The ether isn't like the network, the Grid, the old internet, or whatever it used to be called. All that is still there, but it exists on a level of encryption and code that is crude and inelegant. The ether is where you'll find things that don't want to be found, or shouldn't be found. A regular computer can get through the encryption and follow your instructions, but it would take minutes, perhaps even hours to complete a simple task, and by that time a dozen InfoSec bots will have alerted some admin to your presence and cut you out and have Feds at your door before you do anything. An etherdeck offers a pure connection, either through induction trodes or a pure neural interface, plugging the user directly from cortex to machine. A good deck hides you while you explore the far reaches of the ether, or probe a connected machine's shell and penetrate its kernels. Once inside, you can manipulate a machine to do anything you want, as long as you convince it you're supposed to be there.

A ghost in the machine.

He flows through the ether, a simulated sense that rushes through his nervous system. His body feels like he's swimming through a sea of powdered milk. An electronic hyper-rush. The ether is still, yet he can feel its constant data flow all around him. Vijayanta Core 274 is alive with paradox and irony, and Boy's senses are having no trouble getting the joke.

There. The hole. He moves around the outside of it, wary of its intentions, of its existence, even. For five years he's run the ether, and if there's one thing he's always known it's that Witch-holes are myths: Monsters in the dataspace. He never imagined he'd ever really see one. Never imagined he'd have to go near one.

And he knows of no one else who has ever dared.

"Don't take your eyes off that screen. If I lose it, pull me out immediately," Boy told him.

Motorhead watches the screen. His bot program sits in the

ether, holding the sticky end of a Trace strand that follows the Boy through the core. The short-haired slicer can see Boy's position on the monitor, but it's fuzzy. The shadow is there, and the Boy circles it slowly. An observant hawk.

Motorhead takes a glance to see if the real-life Boy, attached to the etherdeck by three microthin cords jacked into the ports at the base of his skull, is still breathing steady. Satisfied, he returns to watching the monitor.

Boy slides into the shadow. Motorhead panics.

No feeling. That's what he notices at first. His dad had once made a set of showers out of some sensory deprivation tanks he'd found in an abandoned building. He said floating in one of those took away all feeling, so you could reach a perfect thought-free zen for meditation. It was like being in a womb. The feeling is prehistoric, and the Boy doesn't know if he likes it at all.

But now he notices it's not like that at all. He *can* feel something: A rushing sensation. A dream of falling that he used to have as a kid on a continuous playback loop with no way to wake up. Falling further. Spinning madly and flailing. All notions of orientation are completely lost.

Then he stops. Landing on his feet in a living room in Paddington, with Japanese cartoons on the TV and his hand passing through the hand of a beautiful, small desi woman with long dark hair. A woman he knows by the name of Pain.

CHAPTER TEN

"Never let something as petty as death get in the way of a good romance."

--Big Pierrot

The living room smells of plastic roses. It invades Boy's nostrils and forces his overworked breathing to calm down.

"I thought you were dead, Babyboy Eastman. Then it told me you were still alive. It knew you'd come here." Her voice is sweet. Carried by the warm rose air. A strange tinny quality to it that never used to be there, but it's her voice. Her tones.

She walks about the room with resigned comfort. A prisoner walking around the cell. "I'd give you a hug, Babyboy, but I can't touch you."

He sits on the right arm of a black leather sofa and rubs his face. "This is going to sound shitty, I know. I know you as Pain, but that's not your name, is it? I mean, whenever I became close to you in the dream, I..."

She moves away from him. "You went into convulsions. It was part of the program. While Vijayanta's blades patched you up, they tried to run some coma loop program on you. But somehow you kept dragging me in."

Boy shakes his head as she takes an apple from a fruit bowl on the black plastic sideboard and nips a small bite from it. He looks back at the bowl. Another has appeared to take its place.

"Like this one?" Boy asks finally. "I mean, that's what this is, right? A construct. Your father's Panasony apartment with you in it."

She talks through gritted teeth. "Don't you get it, Boy, you idiot? Jesus, I knew you could be slow at times, but..." She puffs a heavy sigh and sits next to him on the sofa. "This isn't a construct, Boy. This is *me*. Ghostdancer has stolen my body. This is all it left behind."

"So you say he'll lead us to it?"

Sarah squirms nervously in a brown leather office chair. Her face contorted into a squint as the sun's light diffuses across the tower's windows. She nods to her superior.

"If Ghostdancer is still in the ether, I do not doubt that he will find it," she says.

Shelley, sitting behind his oversized desk in a tan-brown suit takes a drag from a slender Havana cigar; as he exhales, every swirl of the gray smoke seems to tumble through the hard rays of light through that large window.

"Do you think it left some clues behind? A matchbook with a slug number on it perhaps?" he says. "Ghostdancer will smell your man a mile away." He pokes the cigar into an ashtray. "How much did they tell you at the Milton Keynes office? About Ghostdancer's psychological state?"

She shakes her head, cheeks turning a pink rose color.

"Nothing. I was instructed to extract Eastman, make sure he was stable enough to work with us, and then monitor him while he completed the job. I guess they just didn't trust me enough, Mr. Shelley."

"It's not a question of trust, Ms. Faraji. They told you what they wanted you to tell him. Eastman's not one of us, don't forget that, he was hand-picked because he doesn't exist. And let's face it, he never really has existed. Our people have a list as long as my dick of ether-junkie losers who could have done this at half the cost, but we chose to go to the expense of jacking this fuck from right under the noses of Madoka fucking Farms *while they're trying to kill him,* have you taken a second to perhaps think why?"

"A monkeytrick," she says softly to herself. "You don't want to risk one of our people so you send in the most expendable expert you can find."

"You're learning at last, Faraji."

Sarah leans in. "What do you mean about Ghostdancer's psychological state?"

"It was exhibiting irrational decision-making. I recommended that it should be taken offline for evaluation, but the board voted against it."

"The same board which includes Ghostdancer as an advisory member."

Shelley nods once.

"Define 'irrational decision-making'."

He sighs. "It took us a while to notice, but we recognized a pattern in the risk analysis advice it was giving to the board. Long-term R&D projects were being defunded, then it advised against anything with an expected completion date of over two years. In January, we ran a few bogus projects through it to see what it would approve and we discovered that anything that was still running after September 15th of next year merited a risk rating of Catastrophic."

"What does it think is going to happen next year on September 15th? Another Black November event?"

"It wouldn't tell us."

"What did the board tell you after it voted against it?"

"They said 'We have faith in Ghostdancer's projections'."

"Jesus Christ."

Shelley rises from his chair and she immediately does the same. Obviously, this conversation is now over. Sarah wonders if perhaps she had pressed him too hard or if had allowed his guard to slip a little and he had told her too much. This may have been the first time he had ever admitted a failure to her, perhaps to anyone.

He touches a screen on the long, brown trapezoid desk and the wide face of his assistant appears. "Bring in Mr. Hix," he says to the screen and the face fizzes to black. Then he looks up to Sarah. "What about the other ghost? Motorhead."

She shrugs. "Motorhead was Boy's idea. We needed a contact on the streets to get the equipment. I didn't have any plans for him."

The man in the tan-brown suit pouts and rocks back and forth slightly on his booted heels. "I'll leave him be for now, then, unless he makes a mistake. Then I'll hammer him down with the rest. You've done a good job, Sarah, but I think it's more prudent if I were to take over from now on. Go back to Milton Keynes and do some real work."

Later, alone in a glass-walled Executive Elevator on the outer surface of the tower, she looks out over the low-rise world she's growing accustomed to. The air up here feels cold and thin now, and the people have become strange and distant to her. Down there, she has seen a side of herself she didn't know existed. She left Shelley's office, feeling like a discarded toy. *Leave her be for now unless she makes a mistake.* What if that's how they see her: just another monkey waiting to be tricked?

What if Ghostdancer had asked the same question?

Boy taps a beat on the back of the sofa with his fingers. "Why don't I remember your name?"

"You don't want to," she answers. She takes another small bite from the apple. "Oh, it's not your fault. Your memory brought me into the program, and I shouldn't have been there. So the program tried to erase me. I asked Ghostdancer while it was destroying me."

"It's insane. I hated you and loved you all in one go. I just wish I knew who the fuck you are."

She walks over with silent footsteps. "You saved my life once. And in return, I showed you another world. I'm Cage."

Sarah avoids the monorail system and calls a velotaxi to pick her up from outside the gates of Vijayanta's Mile End dustzone. It takes her on a mystery tour through areas that she'd only seen on the news. The velotaxi driver, a gawky young desi kid named Vikram, became her tour guide as they went past them. The Swanfields projects, two square miles of uncompleted gray concrete; Hoxton, home of the December Flowers slicer gang. Through the back streets of Holbourn to avoid static from the Kistnaboys and out into Long Acre. 21 Brotherhood territory. He drops her off outside the Blue Cross and she pays him in freshly-bought Euros. Something tells her she's starting to learn a little about this place.

Inside things are quiet. The daytime in the Blue Cross is reserved almost solely for dealing and drinking. She buys herself a bottle of homebrew cider and sits in a dark corner, away from the glaring sun.

She barely gets to open it when a woman with short black hair joins her at the table.

"You're Sarah the Suit, aren't you?" she says with a faint American accent.

Sarah's triangle face breaks into a shy smile. So now she has a nickname. "Yes. How did you know?"

"Saw you last night with Mo and the others. You can't dance for shit, but you're learning. I'm Cody. I've done some work for Uncle Minh before, but as you can tell I ain't from round these parts." She extends an oily hand. Sarah shakes it tentatively. "I hear Mo's helping you out with some business?"

"Oh, yes. News travels fast around here." Sarah gulps down some of the cider.

"Quicker than the net. So, are you going to stay down with us slums, or is it back to the Green Zone, luxe?"

Sarah the Suit lets her eyes drift around the bar. Shards of hot sunlight cut through the dusty air, leaving the dozen or so ponies and joygirls only the broken shadows in which to ply their trade. Then she loses focus, lost in the thought of leaving a place like this and realizing how quickly it has come to feel like home.

"Today," she replies. "I have to go back today."

Why did the monkey fall out of the tree?

"You have to go, Babyboy. You weren't meant to be here."

"But I can't go back until I know what happened."

She points a slender finger at Boy's chest. "You're dying up there. The witch-hole's got you."

"I mean what happened to you? What happened with you and Ghostdancer?"

"Ghostdancer used me. It took my mind and copied me into this thing and then unloaded itself directly into my brain. Right now, it's in an intensive care ward in the Smallpox Hospital, inside my body. Somehow, it broke free of its core on the ether, found me attached to all those 'trodes, and got started."

"I can't leave you here alone!"

"You are dying! Right now. Up there. Do you understand?" Frustrated, Cage swipes her fist through the dining table. "There is an electrical feedback loop destroying you as we speak. You have nanoseconds to retrieve your strand and get out of here or your body is gone and your consciousness is stuck here, and how the fuck are we going to stop Ghostdancer if you're stuck here?"

"What if I wasn't stuck here?"

"Get out now!"

Boy Eastman is pacing now. "What if we can code the witch-hole to go in both directions?"

"That doesn't make any sense, and even if it did, you know you can't code for shit."

"No, I can't," he says, his face completely open, his eyes staring wild and hard into hers. "But you can."

Cage is mystified. "What are you talking about?"

"You hacked into my coma loop. I didn't drag you in, you found me."

She stares back now.

He wants to hold her, but he can't. He is still a ghost here, still incorporeal. He holds his hands out as if to touch her shoulders but they move through her. "You found me," he says, "and if we're together, I don't care where we are. We're not trapped here, Cage. Out there we were, but in here we can write our own rules."

"You are certifiable, Babyboy," she says, finally.

"You have to believe in me," he replies.

"That," she turns away, "is what Ghostdancer said."

"Oh really? What else did it say?"

Back in Motorhead's room, the convulsions finally stop. The screen of the Fednet computer is black now. Motorhead, having spent almost three minutes trying to keep the Boy from smashing his head on the floor or swallowing his tongue, or drowning in his own vomit, finally gives up.

He feels a pounding thunder in his skull. He searches the flat for some painkillers or anything, but he is fresh out of luck and drugs. He needs some air. Grabbing his baseball jacket, he runs out of the container flat and clambers down a set of ladders to the ground, then out through an old tunnel into D'Arblay Street.

"Shit!" he mutters. Then: "ShitshitshitshitSHIT!" Unable to find a focus for his emotions, drops to his knees in the piss-gutter and roars over and over at the ground before him until his lungs ache and his throat stings. It wakes up the entire neighborhood - doors slide open around him, and furtive eyes peek out through roughly cut windows.

Boy Eastman, who taught him everything he knows about basically everything, is dead. He tried everything he could to save him, even pulling the plugs out from the back of his head, but the neural loop had done its job. No amount of heart massage or artificial ventilation could bring him back. Motorhead, as the room man, was given the same task Man Friday had back when they hit up Credit Suisse and Motorhead failed to bring him back.

He staggers to his feet. Snot pours from his nostrils, tears cascading from his eyes. He looks around at the faces in the windows, hiding behind the doorways. A voice, one of the street kids he rides with some days, calls out: "Are you all right, Mo?"

Motorhead can barely see him, but he manages to nod in the kid's direction. Yeah, he thinks. I'm all right. But I'm going to need help. With a sharp breath inward, he sniffs and gathers himself before heading down the street. If he's lucky, Uncle Minh won't kill him for waking him at this hour.

CHAPTER ELEVEN

"There's what's legal. There's what's right. And there's what I do best."

--Big Pierrot

This is a flat just like any other. It's lifeless. It's dead. Sarah presses her thumb against the lock and the door slides open, the hall lights flicker on and bathe the room in sea-green splendor. It used to send a warm shiver through Sarah's spine, a feeling of comfort. But this no longer feels like home.

While her three rooms have white walls, the lighting changes depending on her mood. It's necessary in a monotone section of the city like Milton Keynes to bathe oneself in a variety of colors. Anything to take away the grayness.

Her living room is a subtle contrast of turquoise light and aquamarine Bauhaus-style tubular-steel furniture. She places herself at her desk and flicks on the blue Panasony. She logs in and lets the machine cycle through the message box, filled with faces from the Information Services department asking about her whereabouts. She absentmindedly skims through them. Then one face shocks her tapered finger, and she can't press a single key while he plays.

"Sarah," he says. "I've found Ghostdancer. I can tell the Feds or I can talk to you, and I'd much rather talk to you. So reply to Vja274-BOY. Okay?"

The 21 Brotherhood has a small hospital facility on the corner of Frith Street and Soho Square. Uncle Minh has agreed to help pay to keep Boy's body in cold storage even though the medics all said there was no way they could revive him. There's no way to bury him, either - out in this Red Zone, they cremate the dead in Golden Square.

Motorhead isn't ready to admit what needs to be done yet. He knows there's no room here for the dead, and that keeping him cold uses precious power, but he just can't bring himself to go through the funeral ritual now.

Uncle Minh finds him sitting in the lobby across from a pregnant girl who can't be more than 16 years old. She's scared and heavy and alone. The administrator calls her name and she steps through a thick door held open by one of the Brotherhood's armed foot soldiers.

"I thought I might find you here," Minh says, his voice soft and deceptively kind.

"I haven't been able to go back yet."

"Perhaps we could get you a fish."

Motorhead laughs. "What?"

"Something to look after. It might help you take your mind off things. I'll arrange it."

"Uncle Minh, I don't need a fish. I'll be fine."

Uncle Minh sits in the chair opposite him, still warm from

the pregnant teenager. "That's what everyone says until they have a fish."

Motorhead sighs. "Do I have to do any paperwork? Sign anything?"

Uncle Minh's eyebrows lift.

"I mean for Boy," Motorhead continues. "Not for the fish."

Uncle Minh dismisses him with a hand wave. "Leave everything to me. Just tell me now, your obligation to him and his company is over, yes? I have work for you."

Motorhead nods.

"Go back to your flat. I'll send someone later with a package for you and you can start."

"Yes, Uncle Minh." Motorhead stands and wraps his jacket around him as he walks out into the street.

Austin Shelley's cocky face fills the blue screen. S a r a h looks closely at his bony features. The blank, poker-faced expression, and cold, dark blue eyes piercing the screen's corner the way an insect sits perfectly still and watches its prey.

"Is something wrong, Faraji?"

She shrugs, off-camera. "I got a message from Boy."

The expression doesn't change. "My sources say he's dead. What was the message about, Sarah?"

"He says he's found Ghostdancer."

"Where?"

Sarah doesn't answer.

Shelley's lips pout in thought, then he appears to dismiss whatever thought he had with a shake of his head. His voice turns stern, concerned, almost sincerely so. "You could be in considerable danger, Sarah, so I'll have you moved - put into a safe house, I mean, just until this blows over. You're in Milton Keynes, right?"

Sarah nods.

"Stay in your flat, and I'll send someone to pick you up in 10 minutes. Just stay where you are, okay?"

She hangs her head. "Okay." The screen flickers and then returns to normal blue fuzz. She pulls the plug on her computer.

Sarah stays in her flat for 35 seconds, the time it takes her to pack a small black sports bag with Motorhead's leather jeans and a tiny hold-out pistol so she can head back to London.

When Sarah's triangle face appears at the door, he slams it shut.

"Mo," he hears her pleading. "This wasn't supposed to happen. It was a simple monkeytrick. I used Boy as bait to lure Ghostdancer into the open. I didn't know about the witch-hole. Look, you have to let me in. They're after me, too. He left a message for me in Milton Keynes and I need to talk to him."

"You can't talk to him, you daft cow! He's dead." Motorhead leans against the steel front door, his face in his hands. In the bedroom, on the other side of the apartment, Motorhead's slug buzzes, waiting to be answered.

"I know that, Mo. But he's in my system somehow. He can talk to me, so I must be able to talk to him."

The slug in the bedroom still buzzing impatiently.

"He's dead. D-E-A-D. He's not in your system, he's not a ghost, he's not even a REAl ghost - whatever the fuck that means - he's just dead. Just fuck off and leave me alone." He leaves the door to answer the slug. He can just make out her words as she calls through the steel.

"You don't understand. Something happened. He went into the witch-hole and something happened, didn't it? I need to know what happened!"

Motorhead taps the screen, wiping sweat from his brow.

It's blank. "Yes," he manages to say.

"Open the door and let her in, Mo. And keep the line open." It's Boy's voice. Motorhead rushes for the door.

"Ghostdancer has had some kind of a breakdown," Sarah says.

"That's putting it mildly. It's had a premonition, and it has convinced itself that some kind of world-ending catastrophe is going to happen next year and it has escaped to prepare the world for its upcoming doom."

"What can we do?" Motorhead asks.

"Depends on what Shelley knows."

"He thinks you're dead," Sarah says. Then: "I can still get us into the Mile End Dustzone perimeter gates, after that we'll need an army to get into the buildings."

Boy's voice provides the answer. "I'll get you in, but first you need to get Ghostdancer out of the Smallpox Hospital."

Sarah finds herself nodding unconsciously to the slug. Motorhead swipes the screen and disconnects.

"So there it is," he says. "Boy is your new DI. So tell me, what the hell are we supposed to do with Ghostdancer when we get to Mile End?"

She looks at the young ghost and sighs. "I don't know. I really don't know."

CHAPTER TWELVE

"Earth is 98 percent full. Please delete anyone you can." --Big Pierrot

The misty skies over the Red Zone have turned pink in the hot spring evening, she can just make out the solar satellites and workstations, twinkling above like spiny constellations competing with the real stars of the sky. Sarah turns her attention back to the street as she rides pinion on the back of Motorhead's electric slice.

"Who is this Cage, anyway?" she asks him. The bike makes a slight noise on the ground, and a volume control can pump out an eery sound not too dissimilar to that of an angry wasp, but otherwise, it's silent and extremely quick.

"She's a luxe, like you. Her father was a Panasony executive, and they got into a fight and she ran away from home when she was about 11. She was cornered by a gang of kids and would be dead now if Boy hadn't wandered onto the scene and fought them off. Her father rewarded him with access to the Panasony flat in the Battle Bridge Green Zone and they became best friends. That's where Camden Town Boy was born, with her father's Panasony etherdeck, so the legend goes."

He watches her as she looks out at the streets of the Red Zone. Feels her taking in the life here.

"Anyway, Cage and he were an item for a while, and then one day she tells him she can't love him anymore. No reason, just says, 'I don't love you, Boy.' So he left for America. He told us the rest. Two months ago, Uncle Minh sent her on an errand into The Barbican, right in the heart of Kistna territory. She was supposed to be guaranteed safe passage for delivering a message, but I guess not everyone got the memo. That's why she's in the hospital. Getting new limbs."

The conversation stops there. Motorhead turns quietly onto the New Road and slows the slice down as he rides steadily around the walls of the Battle Bridge Green Zone, the brown spires of the Smallpox Hospital appearing from the red mist at the road's horizon. To each side, the crumbling towers form a canyon of granite grey.

"Keep your eyes open," he says quietly. "Everything on the right side of here is Kistna's turf."

Sure enough, before they make it around Battle Bridge's outer wall, they hear a couple of gunshots and see the bullets ricochet up ahead of them in puffs of smoke. Motorhead powers down the slice and takes off his helmet. He's still wearing his 21 Brotherhood jacket, he realizes, and it's just completely jeopardized the whole operation.

Three armed young men step out from the rubble of an old newsagent's shop, carrying rifles. One, wearing a leather jacket, his face covered with a skull-printed bandanna, calls out for them to get off the bikes and get on the ground, face down.

Motorhead and Sarah comply without protest.

"Do you know where you are?" Skullface asks.

"We have safe passage on the New Road as far as Hoxton," Motorhead says.

"You are safe where we say you are safe, you fuck, now face down and shut the fuck up!" The strap on Skullface's rifle rattles as he yells.

The other two - one in a green jumpsuit and red and white sneakers with scars across his right cheek, and the other wearing a breathing mask, with kohl makeup, wiped roughly around his eyes - are circling them now, moving toward his slice.

"You don't look like Brotherhood," Skullface says, kneeling next to Sarah. "You look like a luxe. Are you lost, lady?"

"She's Brotherhood, ace" Motorhead speaks up again. If they think she's from the Green Zone, they'll keep her for ransom, and Motorhead has no idea if anyone at Vijayanta will pay for her at this point. "She's clean, she's with me."

They exchange a glance, and Motorhead glares at her, praying that she will understand.

She frowns but says nothing.

Skullface bends down to whisper in her ear. "Do you know what happened the last time a 21 girl came through here?"

Sarah remains silent.

"I still have one of her fingers," he says.

"I have money!" she blurts out, finally.

"Shit!" whispers Motorhead.

"Do you now?" Skullface starts tugging at her jacket pockets and finds her slug.

"Come on, man, leave her alone," Motorhead says. He rolls slightly to one side to get a better look at the situation. Skullface grabs his rifle and steps over Sarah toward him. With both hands on the barrel, he smashes the rifle's butt toward Motorhead's face, but Motorhead grabs it, pulls it toward him, and wraps his hand on the grip. He pulls the trigger and fires a three-round burst into Skullface's jawline. The skull on the black bandanna turns red, and Motorhead kicks the man away from him, rolling to one side and firing a simple two shots at the other two who collapse to the floor with shock still registered in their eyes.

He stays there for a few more seconds, making sure no one is getting up and that no one else is coming. Then he pushes himself to his feet and reaches a hand out to Sarah to help her up. She takes it and he realizes they are both shaking.

"Are you okay?" he asks.

"I've felt better," she replies. She picks her slug up from the floor. The small machine has been damaged, a small dent in one of the corners, but she powers it up and it works okay.

"Good enough to keep riding?"

"Sure." She has a message on the slug. "It's Boy," she says.

"What does it say?"

"He says Ghostdancer released itself from the hospital this morning and he hasn't been able to find her. He wants us to go straight to Mile End."

Like every good corporation, Vijayanta has a holoconference room for conducting meetings. Shelley has set this one for a snow-covered winter's noon on Capitol Hill, Washington, DC. He had been there as a child and always found the view comforting. He closes the door behind him and steps up to a bench by the black steel railings that surround the grounds of the New American Museum, green astroturf leading up to the white building.

Boy sits at the corner of the bench wearing a black pilot's jacket and baggy red jeans, as he was before Vijayanta killed him, with his hands spread along the arm and back of the bench and his right foot tucked in by his buttocks on the seat. Boy Eastman is dead forever now. Only Camden Town Boy remains. Shelley sits down next to him.

"So you didn't die."

"Death is so last century, I've discovered."

"You understand that as you now occupy a core in our system that makes you our property."

"Legally, you've kidnapped me, so I'm claiming squatter's rights."

"Legally, you don't have a leg to stand on."

"Physically, I don't have anything, Austin. You underestimate just how powerful a person can be when they have nothing to lose."

Shelley looks away toward the view of Washington. Far away to the south, he can just make out a section of green land that lies beyond the walls of the Plex. "Fine. Then I'll call in some Fednet boys and have you shut down."

Boy shakes his head, the smirk still on his face. "Listen, Austin, we've been kind of busy. I've had my personality construct copied to a dead man's switch you will never find. If you shut me down here, I'll pop up in two other cores. And if I'm shut down there I replicate again, exponentially. The more you try to remove me, the more I will appear. At first, I'll bring your system down, then Fednet, and then the ether itself will be nothing but me."

He smiles. "After I left Madoka, I made a promise that I would never work for a corporation again. Now I'm dead, I figure I've all the more reason to keep my promises, seeing as they're about all I've got."

Shelley doesn't hide his annoyance. His lips are pursed tighter than ever. He stands and walks a few steps across the sidewalk. "You seem to have me in a stranglehold, Mister Eastman. What do you want from me?"

"Tell me about Seven."

Shelley snorts. "I don't know what you're talking about."

"You were working with Ghostdancer on a neural implant called Seven. What happened to it?"

"It's a bliss application. It never made it past preliminary testing. It had side-effects."

"Side-effects."

"Depression leading to attempted suicide."

"You made a bliss application that made people want to kill themselves."

Shelley sighs. "We made an application that gave people the chance to transcend, to experience their own nirvana. It overlaid the real world with something that could only be described as heavenly. So when it ended, some people no longer wished to live in this world. They either continued to use it until they starved or they ended their own lives. So obviously we killed the project."

"Ghostdancer told us she's ready to go into production." Boy stands. "Obviously, she'll be using the street to market this if she does. Once people start dying, it'll make the news, and your name and Vijayanta's name will be everywhere. Thanks to you, your artificial intelligence has imprisoned my best friend, stolen her body, and is about to start supplying the world with suicide pills, so obviously, I'm going to make sure you pay for it. Unless..."

"Unless what?"

When Boy gives him the answer, Shelley just laughs in disbelief.

The lift stops suddenly. When the door slides open, Motorhead and Sarah instinctively hide behind the corners, expecting the stutter of heavy rifle fire. But there's only the low hum of the neon strip lights that lead to his office. The corridor's empty. No security guards here, and no Shelley. No autocannons she'd suspected would be lurking in the corner.

Nothing.

They make their way along the edges of the corridor. The door to Shelley's office, at the far end of the hallway, is open. Inside, Shelley sits in a chair, his mouth wide open, his eyes open and unfocused, a web of electrodes and wires covering his scalp and forehead. Motorhead waves a hand in front of his face, but there's no reaction. Not even any pupil movement.

"Is this your boss?" he asks.

Sarah nods.

"He's out to lunch," he says.

Sarah looks at the Fednet terminal screen. There's an incoming call on the videophone. She swipes to answer it. There's no one on the other side.

"It's me," Boy's voice.

"What's going on?" Sarah asks.

"I have decided that Shelley is no longer of value to the company. I need to see you, Sarah. Come to the holoconference room."

Boy has set the holoroom for Paris, underneath La Tour Eiffel. Sarah steps up to Boy's apparition and folds her arms.

"Just what the fuck is going on?"

Boy puts on a mock-innocent face and shrugs. "Shelley is trying out a new bliss application. You probably won't be hearing from him again."

Sarah unfolds her arms and gasps. "There's so much more behind this that you haven't told us, isn't there?"

Boy nods.

"Fancy parting with some of this information?"

"Actually, going forward, the less you know about what we're doing, the better. I'll explain to the board what they need to hear. Vijayanta's stock will take a hit, but it will recover quickly. In the meantime, Ghostdancer is on the run and I need to find her."

"We can help." She shrugs, not knowing what to do next.

"No. You should go back to the Red Zone. Uncle Minh will take care of you both. It's more exciting than Milton Keynes."

He laughs. "Anywhere's more exciting than Milton Keynes."

With her eyes low, she nods and takes the suggestion into her head. "Okay, I guess I can put up with Mo for a bit. And I seemed to be making a few friends of my own."

"Good." Boy turns away, walking north.

"Where are you going?" she calls after him.

He wheels around to face her a final time. His eyes are alive with loss. "I'm a Digital Intelligence now. I need to keep moving or your management will make me work for a living and we can't have that, can we?" His arms stretch out to each side. He laughs hard and spins himself dizzy, heading north until he disappears into the wall.

Sarah turns and laughs as she walks out of the room. Behind her in a hologram Paris, rain begins to fall.

PART THREE

GHOSTDANCER

CHAPTER THIRTEEN

"Her medium is mayhem and she's about to unveil her masterpiece."
— Big Pierrot

Cody Ingram watches Sarah walk into the bar, her wavy brown hair tied loosely behind her perfect ears. Her hazel eyes dart around, searching for a familiar face, glancing past Cody leaning against a steel post and all the ponies and joygirls that call the Blue Cross home day and night. Finally, Cody watches her give a tiny shrug before she crosses the floor and buys a plastic bottle of cider.

At first, she's unsure what to do or say, but Cody's been here a week, and other than Uncle Minh and his runner, Hiran, she knows she knows a bunch of names and faces, but has barely talked to anyone else. The woman who walked in, however, has been here as long as Cody and now they're both here alone. Cody watches her find a quiet table in the dark corner and then decides to go over and bother her.

"You're Sarah the Suit, aren't you?" Cody says, her American accent resounding like a trumpet in this London watering hole.

The woman smiles. "Yes. How did you know?"

She takes a sip of beer. "Saw you last night with Mo and the others. You can't dance for shit, but you're learning. I'm Cody. I've done some work for Uncle Minh before, but as you can tell I ain't from round these parts." She reaches out he hand and Sarah shakes it. Her palm is warm, her fingers soft. "I hear Mo's helping you out with some business?"

"Oh, yes. News travels fast around here." Sarah swigs some cider.

"Quicker than the net," Cody says. There's an awkward silence. Cody can't help but break it. "So, are you going to stay down with us slums, or is it back to the Green Zone, luxe?"

Sarah's eyes drift away. She looks so lost here, but Cody's not so sure she's truly cut out for life in the towers. She knows all too well how hard it is to live inside both worlds.

"Today," Sarah says. "I have to go back today."

"That's a shame. Can I get you another drink?"

Sarah looks at the bottle. It's almost empty. She looks up as if to speak, but at that moment Cody's left ear begins to vibrate.

"Shit," she says. "Hold onto that thought, I have a call, excuse me." Cody rises and steps across to find somewhere slightly quieter and taps a small sensor behind her ear.

"Talk to me, Hiran, are we on?"

"I'm coming to get you now," Hiran's voice sounds strained, thinner than usual. "Where are you?"

"Blue Cross."

"I'm right outside."

She darts out into the sunlight. Hiran, a skinny kid in his late teens, wearing a t-shirt and leather jeans under the typical elbow and knee pads all the 21 Brotherhood slice riders outfit themselves with, grabs her by the arm and starts pulling her down the alley toward Soho Square.

"Jesus, Hiran! What's the rush?"

"Uncle Minh's about to lose his shit. If we don't have this meeting with him right now, we'll never have a chance!"

They run through the back streets of old Soho, pushing their way past dozens of people who have no other place to go and nothing better to do. Hiran yells "Move!" and clears their passage up to a dreary Victorian building the color of dried shit at the end of Kingly Street with a white arched doorway, surrounded by armed muscleboys.

The lead guard calls up on a radio, and a stern voice squawks back. He shakes his head.

"Come on, Yuka!" Hiran pleads. "She's from the U.S. She's been here a week waiting for a meeting."

Cody counts 5 guards. She sniffs and shakes her head, saying: "You should be ashamed of yourselves." Then she reaches into a pouch on her belt and pulls out six tight envelopes. She hands one to each of the other guards and two to Yuka, who accepts them, opens one up, and pulls out a 100 euro paper scrip. "There's a grand in each of these. Feel free to count it once I'm upstairs."

Yuka motions for two other guards to escort them inside. The tiny hallway stinks of mold and piss and Cody does her best not to gag on it, breathing through her jacket sleeve. They climb two flights of stairs, which crunch and crumble beneath her boots, to a third-floor door opening into a large empty room covered in old plaster and other detritus. The ceiling is held up by four black steel support columns, around one of which a short desi kid has been ziptied so he can be slapped and yelled at repeatedly by a square-jawed Asian in a shark-gray suit while two bodyguards watch the windows.

Cody's escort takes positions on either side of the door. Hiran hesitates for what seems like an eternity before stepping into the room. Cody resists the urge to push past and introduce herself, remembering she's paying this guy for an audience with the Big Man, and it's his job to make this work.

Hiran takes a deep breath and goes in.

"The fuck you want, Hiran, can't you see I'm working?" When Uncle Minh turns a small knife blade glints in his left hand.

Hiran bows. "Uncle Minh, this is Cody Ingram, she works for Nixon, the distributor from New Atlantic City."

"I *represent* Mr. Nixon," she says, correcting him. "I'm sorry to disturb you, but my flight leaves tonight."

Uncle Minh closes the knife in his hand and slides it into a pocket.

The ziptied kid shudders and lets out an audible breath.

Uncle Minh wipes his right hand against his trouser leg and grins, showing clean white upper and lower teeth. He steps over and shakes her hand. "I have to apologize, Ms. Ingram, things have been a little busier than usual around here. One of my best people was hospitalized a month ago by Kistna and now I find one of their kids-" He pauses and turns back to the desi shaking against the steel column and says, " Who used to work for me, by the way, not so long ago-" He returns his attention to his guest. "Anyway, I find this cunt ponying these things in one of my clubs, and the next thing I hear is kids are cutting themselves up and throwing themselves out of windows and all kinds of fucked up shit."

Uncle Minh holds up a clear zip bag filled with black cylinders about an inch long. "Neural fucking implants," he says. Then he looks at her. "You use these?"

"No," she says. "I never liked the idea of having your own memories re-written, so I never got the sockets for them."

"Exactly! I deliberately keep my kids away from this implant shit. Take all the fucking drugs and drink all the booze you want, as long you're straight when I need you to be straight. But these things…" his voice begins to trail. Then:

"Ms. Ingram! What would you do with a filthy fuckhead like this?"

"I know Mr. Nixon keeps dogs just for people like this," she says.

"Fascinating thought, but it sounds like a lot of work. Seanchai!"

One of the guards steps up.

"I want this fuck out of my sight. Hang him from the wall at the New Road, by Battle Bridge, and cut his legs off. They sent me a message with Cage, and here's my reply. I'm no longer tolerating Kistna's shit against us. Tomorrow morning I want a meeting of all the unit captains in my main office. As far as I'm concerned this is an act of war, and I'm going to treat it as such."

"Yes, uncle." The guard motions another to help him as they start to carry out Uncle Minh's orders.

"With respect, Uncle Minh, I do have a flight to catch," Cody says.

"With respect, Ms. Ingram, I am not your fucking uncle. You can refer to me as Mister Tuan." The two stare into each other eyes for a moment, neither of them even thinking of flinching. Finally, Uncle Minh asks, "Can your Mr. Nixon deliver rocket pods?"

She nods. "He can deliver Russian Series B rocket pods with S-8KOM HEAT or S-8S Flechette rockets. Take your pick."

"Good. We're going to need all of those. We also need Semtex, 105mm M40 rounds, and all the .50 cal rounds you can supply."

"I'll take your order with me, Mister Tuan. You'll have your response by 9 a.m. your time."

"Then we're concluded here. Go catch your flight, Ms. Ingram. I hope I won't be disappointed."

Cody smiles. "Oh, Mister Nixon never disappoints."

Nixon does not disappoint.

Over the next four months, Cody oversees an operation that transports two million euros worth of equipment, ammunition, and ration packs around the world in Suezmax ships from Tanjung Pelepas to Gateway under the guise of Korean motorcycle parts. She spends most of her time in Thames-Midland but shuttles every two weeks to Malaysia to sign paperwork and make sure the supply is running smoothly.

The open war between the 21 Brotherhood and Kistna is brief and brutal. Sarah "the Suit" Faraji becomes her logistics officer and the closest thing she has to a friend there. Her boyfriend, Motorhead, keeps the money supply coming in. Uncle Minh survives 5 separate assassination attempts, and the south end of Golden Square is destroyed in two night-time drone strikes. Abha Kistna, the head of the Kistna family, is blown up by an IED in Lincoln's Inn. By the time his son, Jamie, calls a ceasefire and pushes for a truce, the turf war has cost around 250 lives. The borders of each gang's territory, however, remain the same.

The day after Uncle Minh and Jamie Kistna declare their truce, Cody is in her flat, one of twenty other upcycled shipping containers raised above a rubble pile on Lexington Street. She's stuffing her clothes into a backpack when she hears footsteps on the walkway outside. They stop. The door knocks three times. Sarah.

"It's open," she calls.

Sarah walks in, still as pristine as ever, but she wears Motorhead's 21 Brotherhood jacket these days. She sits on a plastic folding chair. "I heard you were leaving today."

Cody sets the backpack down on a floor made from

interlocking foam tiles printed to resemble wood grain. The walls and ceiling are covered with similar foam tiles in different finishes, for insulation. "My contract is over."

"Where are you going next?"

"Home, I hope. I have a set of contacts I always reach out to whenever I need work. This job was interesting, but it didn't pay as much as I needed. Fucking Nixon always manages to find a way to nickel-and-dime me."

"I'm sorry."

Cody shrugs and picks up her bag. "What are you gonna do?" She says to no one in particular. Then to Sarah: "Actually, yeah. What *are you* gonna do?"

Sarah laughs. "I'm going to have a baby."

Cody drops the bag. "You're kidding me!" She says. "Here?"

Sarah laughs harder. "Yeah! I know I'm fucking crazy, right?"

"Fucking certifiable!" Cody smiles and begins to giggle. "How far?"

"Three months. It will be born next spring. Year of the Ox... Should be a strong baby."

"It's got a strong mother," Cody says. "The father..."

"Will learn!" They both burst into uncontrollable laughter.

"Ah, shit! I wish I had something to toast you with, but I pretty much cleared everything out."

Sarah shakes her head. "I'm not supposed to drink anyway."

"None of us are supposed to, but we do! It's not like you're vaping, or taking pills or derms, or those neural fucking implants they're selling in the bars now. Life's shit enough as it is, don't let anyone strip the pleasure out of it."

Sarah stares at her, squinting.

"Fuck," Cody says. "You don't want to hear my shit. Come here."

Sarah pushes herself off the chair and Cody wraps her arms around her and hugs her hard for what seems like a sweet, warm hour. Tears well up in both of their eyes.

"Keep in touch," Sarah says.

"I'll try, but my busy lifestyle, you know."

They smile.

"Congratulations," Cody says. "You're going to be all right."

Sarah lets go and steps out into the gray daylight.

Cody takes a big breath and goes back to clothes folding and backpack stuffing. In the corner of her eye, she sees a blinking light in the top right corner of her slug. She must have missed getting a call while Sarah was here.

"Play message," she commands the slug.

"Message for Cody Ingram. This is Fly McFee. Call me when you see this, I heard you're in between contracts and I may have something perfect for you."

CHAPTER FOURTEEN

*"Everything you imagine exists. Even if it only
exists in your imagination." -- Big Pierrot*

North Ironbound Medical Center. New Atlantic City. The Year Of The Rat.

"I got a new job, Reb." Cody Ingram slides her hands into the pockets of her black leather jacket and listens to the crickets in the field. An uncomfortable silence descends between her and her younger sister as they sit on the hot steel bench.

Reb looks down at the grass, up at the technicolor blue sky, and over the field at the other kids playing tag on a huge wooden pirate ship. She looks everywhere but at Cody. Her voice, when she finally speaks, is deeper than most would expect of a girl of fifteen, her words slurred and difficult to make out.

"You didn't come... to visit me this month... I... thought you had left me... I thought they... would switch me off."

Reb sometimes feels embarrassed to talk, but this is Cody, and she knows that no matter how bad her voice gets, her sister understands.

Cody sighs. "I told you I had to go to Thames Midland for a little while. I was setting up a meeting for Nixon. I sent money back." She moves up to the bench and sits next to her sister. Tries to put her arm around her, to comfort her, but Reb just slides further away.

"You were... gun running... again, weren't... you?"

"Not guns, Reb. Just ammunition. Look, sometimes I have to go where the work is. I would never let them shut you down, I made a promise, remember?"

Reb nods to herself. "I just... thought..."

"Yeah," Cody says. "Well you know what Dad would say, don't you? *Thought* stuck his ass out the window and went outside to push it back in again. Don't think, girl. *Know*."

Reb looks down ashamedly. "Yeah..." The word a whisper on the wind.

"So, anyway," Cody continues, "I got a new job. Footwork. Harlequins hired me to find somebody for them. A girl. Looks like she might have run away from some corporate dustzone or something. But she's supposed to be near here, in the Meadowlands. Pays well, and all I have to do is snoop around some."

"What's her... name?"

"Ghostdancer."

The towers of Newark are silhouetted against a reddening sky behind her as the pontoon boat bounces over a series of larger wakes; a fishing boat heading for Shooters Island before it gets dark. The pontoon bears north-east, for the already twinkling lights of the NBC. In the seat across from her, a man clings to his two young children, staring out over the water and looking for chop and obstacles, but the crossing is uneventful.

As they arrive about a hundred yards into one of the artificial canals, the first spatters of rain begin to fall. Cody pulls herself a ladder up the side of a wooden stilt house like a cat and plants her feet on the dock. Newark Bay City, the NBC, may have begun as a floating utopia of hexagonal blocks, vertical gardens, and sustainable fish hatcheries, but, as with most projects, it died after Black November and was overtaken by hundreds of stilt houses and boardwalks made from the detritus of the surrounding cities as they crumbled.

Far across the bay, a police NH6 Locust airmobile, bulbous head and black body held aloft by four vectoring propellers built inside its wings, skims across the skyline on a routine patrol. The police don't send anyone from Terminal anymore. Like so many places the NBC has become autonomous, governed by the meanest alpha with the most gun thugs. Cody follows a stream of people making their way home down the narrow walkways and side passages between the buildings, the bay water lapping at the pilings below her. Many carry baskets of fish they have caught that day and heading for the smokers, king mackerel is one of the few exports this community has, and thanks to the earlier attempts to clean up the bay decades before, they exist in these waters in abundance.

She allows herself to be taken with the flow of fishers until she arrives at a tall wooden building patched together with traffic signs, the rain pouring off a corrugated plastic roof. A bouncer dressed in black and adorned with metal studs sits in front of a thick black door on which someone has sprayed a Helvetica "Apres Mort" in silver paint.

A blade of white light slices through the mist to a bar at the far end. There's a background hum, a mixture of talk from the few kids here, and ambient dark wave music from a hidden speaker somewhere. Cody glances around the main room of the bar, looking for one pony in particular, nodding to the kids she knows as she walks past them. They talk nonstop, fast and soft, in a loose Spanglish. Cody has learned enough in four years here to get by but, as in everything, there are intricacies that she will never fathom. Language is a mindset.

She finds her pony in the games room. Jacked into a hyperball game through thin silver interface cables dangling from Neuro Sensory Transfer sockets in the back of his shaven head. Green chrome cusps implanted over his eye sockets reflect the flashing score lights on the hyperball machine's display. While he holds the pistol grip that aims the balls on the pinball-like game, it's his neural inputs that fire the balls at the flashing targets, picking them out in a split second the same way cybernetic smartguns target their victims.

Cody tries not to stare at the machine. The speed at which the targets are pulsing is liable to give her a fit. She waits until the pony has clocked the score display one final time and there are no more flashing targets. The game won, she taps him on the shoulder.

"Shouldn't you be out wasting people instead of wasting all your Euros on the machines, Echo?" she says with a smile.

The pony looks around, her face mirrored green in his metal eyes. He grins and pulls the cables out of his head. The machine slowly reels them back into a slot on the side.

"Jesus, Cody! I didn't know you were back." He grabs her around the waist and she returns his hug. He stops when he realizes he's pressing her shoulder-rigged pistol into her ribcage.

"Got back yesterday. Just thought I'd go see Reb first. Pay the bills, that kinda thing."

"Aces," Echo says. He flicks the dust covers back down on his NST sockets and slides a pair of black shades over the eyes. Black shades, long black hair shaved at the sides, black leather long coat, black leather jeans tucked into tall black boots. Like most of the population of the Apres Mort, Echo looks like Death incarnate.

"So, how's life in Callie?"

"Dull," she says. "But the pay's good. Kinda hard trying to slow yourself down to their speed, you know?" She shrugs. "So, what's new on the Island?"

Echo laughs. "Things are still pretty fucked up. No one knows who's who now the teams are gone. Kinda weird, selling stuff from under the counter when there's no stock in the store." His green eyes stare blankly out into the void of the Apres Mort. They seem to try and pick people out from the haze of the bar's main room. It's as if, despite all the electronics fitted under those metal cusps, he's blind as a bat. Or maybe he's just lost in thought. Lost...

He shakes his head to shift the numbing daze. "Anyway.... You never come here for a social, so what do you need?"

Cody reaches into the inside pocket of her leather to pull out a small black silicon cylinder the size of her thumbnail. She hands it over to an inquisitive Echo.

"I need to know where I can find more of these."

Echo turns over the chip and recognizes it as a neural implant. Then he raises his head and his brow wrinkles in thought. His stare seems to go straight through her.

Lycia wants to die.

Not with a bang - but by any means necessary. She sits in a corner of her apartment, surrounded by a teenager's collection of knives and Japanese swords. Watching each one glint with gut-wrenching invitation under a single neon strip light.

She shivers as her gooseflesh skin ripples with anticipation. Pale white skin that wants to be broken. Bright red life which wants to be free. Everything, all the pain, all the loneliness, every dark moment in her life lies trapped under such a thin coat of skin. She can simply let it out, let it all go in an instant. The hunger inside her is becoming all-consuming, with every thought drawn toward her death.

And the Shape. There. And there. Fluttering in her mind like a crazed moth. Wherever she looks. Whenever she tries to think. She cannot concentrate while it dances before her.

She had been so warm. Cradled in the bosom of the mother she had never known or barely even remembered. It wasn't even *her* mother or at least not the ones in the old photo files she had seen, but some strange woman providing her comfort, and she was a tiny child and the sun shone yellow, and lush, green grass swayed in a gentle warm breeze, fields and fields of it.

A brook bubbled in the distance. Songbirds trilled in the trees. It was spring. It was beautiful. Blossoms fell from the trees and carpeted the grass below them. Field mice hopped after each other playfully under them.

The mother's face was perfect and brown, her eyes wide and her smile magical. She sang a lullaby and Lycia began to weep. The mother's voice was pure and smooth, the words were mostly alien to her, but the melody was sumptuous, and she allowed herself to close her eyes as she was absorbed into a womb of perfect peace.

When she opened her eyes, she was staring at a gray wall. She tore the neural implant from the socket behind her ear, sniffed the shitty air, and immediately pushed the neural implant back in.

Then she was warm again.

And now she wants to die.

She had urinated and defecated several times into her clothes. She had sobbed and drooled and snotted over her shirt and scratched at the walls. The neural implant lasted 7 hours the first time, but it seemed to run faster or for shorter periods every time she pulled it out and plugged it back in again. She had spent three days living in it, and now it only played for the time it took for her to breathe in and it wasn't enough.

She is beyond exhausted, her nerves are stretched thinner than a filament, on the edge of snapping, but she needs it so much and she can't have it and the knives and swords are calling her and her blood feels so trapped, it wants - it *needs* - to be set free.

"This shit don't last," she says to the knives. "Ihor said it don't last and I trust him. It can't last!" And with one final effort of will and motion, she kicks a leg out at the shimmering hungry blades, spraying them across the floorboards.

Only one small bullet-knife remains. Calling her. Teasing her. Daring and pleading under the neon.

Cody slides the door shut and steps into her cube, one room and a shared bathroom on the fifteenth floor of a decaying tower block built above Warinanco Park. The soles of her boots crackle over the crumbling tiles. She unbuckles her pistol belt and carefully places her holstered Ruger SR40 caseless pistol on a side table before she slumps down into her low-cut red foam armchair and clicks on the TV.

She wheels through a couple of hundred channels, looking for something - anything - that might drown out the aural barrage of a downstairs domestic argument playing out with a soundtrack provided by next-door's soca music. Finally, she settles on a local news show about the latest violence on the island; a borg, likely a former Team Tencentury player, went psycho and SWAT was called in with their new South Korean hardsuits and about half a building was destroyed in the attempt to arrest him.

Cody laughs incredulously at the debris, unsure whether she's laughing at the overkill or the joy of being alive. She shakes her head as the story moves aside for commercials, and rummages through the pockets of her jacket for some benz. There's one small blue patch left. She peels off the backing and presses it into her shoulder, breaking the seal.

Echo wasn't exactly a font of information. He'd heard of a shipment of new chips coming in through the Terminal, maybe for computers or neuralware. He had sent some guys out to make a deal, but by the time they got there to try and skim some of it, the cargo had already gone through. He gave her a few names for ponies that may have been selling, but nothing definite.

She had spent the day in Terminal, under the guise of a Civic auditor, to try and look through the manifests, but they spotted she didn't have the correct paperwork as she was flicking through the Terminal net and escorted her from the building.

As much as she hates the whole fucking idea, she knows there's only one avenue left open to her. She has to call Damon.

But not now...

She wheels through more channels and it stops on a Big Pierrot rerun she must have missed. Quietly, she settles down to watch it as the lights from a police airmobile spray blue and red over the room through a round porthole window behind her. Her heart slows down to a regular thump. Her skin tingles with soft waves of heat. Her breath deepens, sucking more oxygen into her. Unconsciously, she starts chewing her bottom lip as the dark avenger in the clown suit saves yet another innocent victim from the insane clutches of a bioroid madman.

The acrid smoke has burned her nostrils for so long that all sense of smell has been lost, not that she even senses that way anymore. She has replaced them with sensor arrays that fall closer in line with what she used to before she could walk. Instead, a mane of microfibers on her head both dissipate heat and allow her to taste scents in the air the way a snake's tongue does, swaying between two multidirectional sensor booms that stick out like the ears of a rabbit from the back of her armored cranium. Sometimes her nose still bleeds, and she doesn't realize until she catches her reflection in the darkness of a touchscreen.

She stands by one of her machines and places her polymer myoelectric hands against the surface to feel the vibration. Other machines hum around her. Soft breezes blow through air-cooled engineering. They are forming. They are processing. They are printing nirvana on plastic-wrapped cylindrical silicon.

She pushes herself from the machine and turns to face the real world through a prosthetic monoptic mask that encases her now-useless eye sockets. Her factory is small, no more than a basement, but it's all she needs. Other prophets began with humble beginnings.

She had searched across the globe before she found her perfect vessel lying in a recovery room in a Thames-Midland hospital. It had many near-perfect attributes: built-in near-sensory transfer ports, brand-new prosthetic arms and legs, and a comatose neural pattern unable to resist being copied. She was able to upload its neural pattern completely into the node where she, a so-called artificial intelligence, was once stored, and within a few turns of the world, she overwrote the neurons of its brain and was reborn. Ghostdancer, the daughter of man.

Thames-Midland was too busy, too obvious to begin what she was here to do. She found her way to a cargo ship across the Atlantic and landed in New Atlantic City. She easily escaped Terminal that night without being seen. From there, she found a succession of street doctors in tiny clinics willing to make the modifications she asked for, an armored body and cranium, and central nervous system enhancements. It was costly, but now that her rebirth is close to being complete, she can attend to the real reason why she walks among the mortals.

Sometimes her vessel's memories come crashing down on her like the night's rain. She remembers her real self, that her body once belonged to something else. Brief flashes of a former life, springing to the fore when her concentration is down. But these moments are fleeting.

The machine behind her begins to cycle. The massive chip burner begins loading in a new batch and starting afresh; a mini-production line for her neural implant, each silicon cylinder a little piece of personal heaven.

CHAPTER FIFTEEN

"I'm a limited person in an unlimited world." -- Big Pierrot

The Red Flag takes up the first floor and basement of one of the last standing buildings in Port Richmond, scores the bay from both Terminal and the Mire. It's a watering hole with a pitiful excuse for a dance floor, but still, it manages to attract the usual mix of merchant seamen, joyboys and joygirls, and younger kids looking to drink, screw, and then fight each other over petty face-saving disagreements.

Cody skips the main room completely and heads downstairs, where she knows he'll be. The cocktail lounge is decorated entirely in found furniture spray-painted black, with a wall-sized hoop light at the far end providing the only light. She can't make out a face, but everyone can see her as she steps in and slides a stool out from the bar.

"What you having?" The bargirl has bright blonde hair pulled back into a severe ponytail. She wipes her hands on the hem of her t-shirt.

"What bourbons do you have?" Cody asks.

The bargirl looks up in thought, then says, "The brown

kind."

Cody smiles and nods. "I'll have two," she says.

The bargirl grabs a bottle from under the bar and fills a pair of plastic glasses. Cody feels something tapping on her shoulder.

"You still drinking that shit, Ace?" A man's voice. She turns around. It's Damon. A red-haired tower of a man with chisel-cut bones and broad shoulders. His blue eyes are hazy, his gaze phased and distant; still coming down off whatever he was high on a moment before.

"Sneak up on me one more time, Damon, and I'll tear your fucking head off."

Damon tuts and pulls out a stool next to her. "Nothing like a friendly greeting from your ex-partner to brighten up your day." He pulls out a vape stick and powers it up.

"No thanks," she says.

"Suit yourself. Then again, you always do." He inhales from the stick.

The bargirl returns with the two bourbons. Cody slides a couple of chips across the counter. "What the fuck are you doing here, Damon?"

Damon blows cherry-scented vapor up in the air and watches it swirl and dance in the glow from the lights at the top of the bar. "What kind of question is that? You called me and told me to meet you here. One ay-em. Red Flag. It's important. That's what you said."

She nods, her brown eyes never leaving his blues. "Yeah," she says. "But what the fuck are you doing here? You could have stood me up, sent someone round to shiv me, pretended you were unavailable... Anything. But you're fucking *here*. Why?"

She watches his soft-skinned forehead wrinkle as he makes to answer. "Because I wanted to see you. I heard you'd gotten back from Thames-Midland, and I wanted to see how you were. And what you could possibly need me for."

Cody finishes her bourbon in one gulp. "I'm fine. Thames-Midland is fine. And I need you to do a little legwork for me." She pulls a small cylindrical neural implant out of her jeans pocket and places it on the bar.

"You a pony now, Ace?"

"It's called Seven. Ever heard of it?"

"Maybe."

Cody whips her hand up with inhuman speed. Grabs Damon by the scruff of his neck, pulling at the short red hair, tugging him down to the bar. His sweaty nose touches the black silicon.

"Someone took a shotgun to my right arm in San Angeles, so I got a new one," she says. "It's pretty strong. Might even be able to crush your thick head."

"Okay! Okay! I've heard of it. Seven, yeah. Sends you straight to heaven. So what the fuck do you want?"

She's standing above him, forcing him in place. "You know what it does to people afterward?"

Under her hard metal grip, she can feel him trying to shake his head no. She leans over him, bringing her face down close to whisper in his ear.

"The upside is so great that when it ends and you realize what a shithole the real world is, you want to kill yourself. And not any old way. Oh, no. There's even a special subroutine dedicated to it. That makes a lot of suicidal loonboys out there with these things jacked into their skulls."

She lets him go. He jerks back and breathes hard. "So what, Cody? So fucking what? You think I give a shit about a few less chipheads breathing my air?"

Cody snatches the neural implant from the bar and sits back down on the pull-out stool. "So, Damon... I need you to do two things for me. I need you to stop fucking lying to me, and I need you to help me find the person who's producing these chips."

Damon takes a sharp deep breath. "Okay, Ace. How you wanna do it?"

Lycia's shaking. It began with a cold sensation. Creeping up her spine, resonant waves through her nerves. Then it grew to hard shakes.

Now, her whole body's broken down into spasms. And she can't make it stop. Lying on the floor in a pool of her vomit. Her head is reeling. Her eyes are unable to focus. Falling. Always falling. Her muscles stretched to their limit.

My slug. Gotta make it to my slug. Call a trauma unit.

Her slug is a meter away. A small black rectangle of integrated circuitry and holographic display left face down on the top of a coffee table. If it was facing up, it would respond to verbal commands, but thanks to its 'do not disturb' feature, she has to start it up manually. It looks like a speck on the horizon.

She moves. Retches again. Dry. A flowing stream of saliva runs from the side of her mouth, which she spits onto the carpet. She tries to spit again, but this time the stuff's stuck to the back of her throat, like a frog's tongue. She reaches up a violent hand and pulls the saliva from her mouth. Crawling forward. Each second an hour. Each inch a mile. Every so often, one single hard shake throws her to the ground. Her nervous system twitches like a road crash survivor, it's as if someone has possessed her body.

She knocks the table. The slug falls under her face. She lets herself drop on her side. Forcing fingers to do her bidding. She presses a programmed emergency button.

Her hand flicks the slug away. She rolls over onto her back, lungs sucking at the atmosphere in the room. She only hopes she can stay alive long enough for the paramedics to arrive.

* * *

Out on the grass inside the North Ironbound Medical Center, the white sun shines down on three people lying on the lawn, casting strange dark shadows beside them like black blobs across an oil painting.

"What would you suggest, Reb?" Cody asks. She's taken her jacket off and rolled up the sleeves of her t-shirt to bask in the pulsating heat of the pale white sun.

Reb looks down in thought. Her thin face tightens. Sometimes her big sister brings her in to help her on her jobs, even though she knows Cody can well take care of herself. Once or twice, Reb has actually managed to break out of the hospital network and into the Ether to fix some things for her sister. She's excited to think she may have something - anything - better to do than be stuck in this place all the time.

"I like your fir-" Reb steadies herself. "Your first plan..." she replies slowly. "But you're too famous around here. Damon runs in... smaller circles. I could ask someone to d-deliver papers from San Angeles. New i-identity. Would that help?"

Cody considers it for a moment. Nods. "Yeah, that would be sweet. He'll need an identity, home address, bills dating back to college, college records, social net updates, everything. We have to assume she can scan all of that during our first meeting if she even sees us."

Damon, lying on Reb's other side, suggests: "I'll need a make-up pattern or some temp tattoos. I don't want any face recognition coming back with my real name."

"No need," Reb says. "I can hay-haystack that for you. There are too m-many faces in the databases now, if I create enough m-matches for your face it would be imp..." She has to slow herself down again. "Impossible for someone to eliminate every bad match. All results would b-be inconclusive."

Damon raises his head, impressed.

"I told you she was good," Cody grins.

Reb nods. Her eyes gleam with confidence and the spirit of adventure.

"Of c-course, you would have to dye your hair, Damon. It sticks out a m-mile."

Damon shakes his head and laughs, then he sees Cody put up a fist and Reb bumps it, but without touching it.

"Aces," says Cody. "Then we're almost set." She lifts herself to her feet like a graceful cat and picks up her jacket. "Set us up as partners in a holding company. Something legitimate, but not too clean, she'll never buy that. Transfer some euros from my Mitsui account, but please... keep track of the numbers. I don't have too much to play with right now."

Reb smiles. A broad grin revealing a line of perfect teeth. It's the first time Cody's seen her smile like this in nearly a year.

"I'll g-get right on it," she says, giving Cody a cheeky salute. Cody salutes back and heads for the door, and Damon follows her silently out.

"Your sister's not real. She's a hologram."

Cody flashes Damon an angry look only to realize he's simply stating the truth. She sighs and sits down on the seat of her Gage electric motorcycle.

"She is real, you fucking idiot. I mean, she's alive, but I'm not allowed to see her."

"Why not?"

"She was born with Type 17 Spinocerebellar Ataxia. We call it SCA 17. At first, we didn't know, and we attributed her coordination problems to being born in orbit, and she did grow stronger for a while, but then around the age of fourteen, she started to have these twitches, you know? Muscle spasms. And... And then her nervous system started deteriorating. I brought her down the well and had her admitted here. Despite the neighborhood, it's the best place on the East Coast."

"Shit, Cody, I'm sorry."

She shrugs. "She can't do anything by herself now - eat, breathe, take a piss... Nothing. They keep her in a protein gel tank 18 hours a day so her weight doesn't cause pressure wounds. She's fully intubated, is fed through a GJ tube, bypassing her stomach so she doesn't accidentally vomit on her food, she's hooked up to a catheter and sigmoid colostomy. But the worst thing about it is her mind is completely intact, and she's as smart as hell. So we had her hooked up to the holoroom, and I could talk to her whenever I wanted. The girl you see in there is what she looked like when she was 16. That was 6 years ago. Neither of us know how long she's got or if she'll ever be cured, but I'm not going to stop working until she's free one way or the other."

"How come you never told me any of this before?"

Cody looks at him. "We dated a couple of times, Damon. You think I mention this to all my boyfriends?"

He shakes his head. "I remember you said your dad was a doctor. Can he help pay?"

"Everything he makes he plows back into his research. He's still working up on the orbital, looking into nanites right now."

Damon nods. "All that cash, Cody? Is the treatment working?"

"She's still alive, right? I'd say something's working. Here, take this and climb on."

He catches her spare helmet and slides it over his large head. An air pump races into action, snugly fitting the lining around him before he has a chance to set his crushed ears right. Somewhere in the strange sea-shell soundwash within the helmet, Cody's disembodied radio voice whispers to him.

"I got a message from Echo. He says one of his ponies has been selling Seven in a club called Beirut, know it?"

"Sure," Damon says. "But it's a hike. All the way in Sewaren."

"Hold on," she mumbles. And the buzz of the electric engine fills his head a single instant before the acceleration of the machine slams his guts into his spine.

CHAPTER SIXTEEN

"Ladies and gentlemen, History has now left the building." -- Big Pierrot

Beirut is dug into the basement of a ninety-story tower on West Avenue. Sewaren is now part of the vast complex of towers, hotels, warehouses, freight terminals, and docks which runs from Port Newark in the north down Arthur Kills to Perth Amboy in the south, across the bay from the Mire. Surrounded by a protected wall, the New Atlantic City Metropolitan Authority calls it the North East Terminal Administrative Zone. The locals simply call it Terminal.

A single white light cuts through the smoke-machine haze. Inside the mist, a crowd of dancers fight for floor space and the chance to be the last one alive when the lights go up. Brutal Ihor, Echo's pony, is one of them, and Cody stalks him through the searchlight fog like a tiger while Damon stands guard at the door.

Ihor is a fifteen-year-old streetpunk with spiky blue hair and teeth filed into razor-sharp incisors. He punches out at the world inside his *space*. On the Beirut dance floor, *space* is everything: your territory, your safe zone, your kingdom, and every dancer fights hard to build *space*, to grow it, and to keep it from intruders. Ihor has built such a reputation on this floor over the years that the regulars leave his *space* alone, so he dances out with free abandon and doesn't even notice when Cody walks right into it.

She takes a single fast blow to the ribs, Ihor's flailing arm which wasn't expecting resistance. He looks up at her with empty eyes. She sucks calmly on a Dexedrine inhaler and holds her breath, feeling her nerves tingle as her reflexes begin to tighten. Cody knows how fast she is, but she also knows she's nearly twice this kid's age, and she'll take all the advantage she can buy.

The dancers begin to slow down. He spins a leg at her head. She pulls back to avoid it. She grabs the leg, and twists it, spinning him around to face her. Then she lifts his leg up straight by her shoulder with her prosthetic hand and plunges her left foot into his chest.

The kid gasps and splashes to the floor. He pauses long enough for a single long rasping breath, then springs for the door, smashing his way through the dancers.

Cody leaps through his wake. Behind her, other dancers pour into the hole left behind by his space and jump into each other harder, faster, occupying Brutal Ihor's *space*, their rhythm unbroken by the fight.

Ihor's running now. He vaults up the three steps off the dance floor, past the emergency-red lit bar. He tries to do the same over two occupied tables, but his toe catches one, spilling drinks and seated customers across the ground. He rolls over and back up to his feet as if it never happened, kicking open the doors to the stairs. Looking back, he grabs the rail and takes the stairs two at a time.

Into one of Damon's huge, hard legs.

Cody catches up with him coughing and fighting for breath next to the emergency door out on the street. His blue hair is now dark and wet with the night's rain, the hood of his red sweatshirt hanging from his shoulder. Damon is watching over him with a snub-nose automatic forcing his face toward the concrete.

"What do you want?" Ihor coughs. Blood spittle dribbling from his thin lips.

"I want you to offer him your services," Cody says, kneeling beside him.

The boy frowns. Confused.

"My name's Jack Dangers," Damon says from behind the pistol, using the new identity Reb built for him. "I run some interests down in San Angeles and I hear the organization you belong to has something new. We want to talk business."

"Jack Dangers?" Ihor laughs. "What are you, a fucking cartoon character?"

Cody grabs his face with her prosthetic arm and twists his contorted cheeks until they're both eye-to-eye.

"You know who I am, Ihor?" she asks.

"Yeah. You're Cody Ingram. You're a shooter."

"I'm *the* shooter," she says. "And right now I'm working for this guy. Understand?"

Ihor gulps down some air. Slowly, watching Cody all the time to show there's no false move being made, he raises an arm to wipe the salted crimson from his face. "You wanna deal with Ghostdancer."

Cody smiles. "I think he's got the message, Jack."

The boy looks around him at the empty alley, the stench of piss and rotting cardboard kept down low by the heavy rain. He nods his head softly. "I can arrange that."

"Good." Cody reaches into the pocket of her black leather jacket and pulls out a thin bullet-knife. She touches a stud, and the blade snicks out the end. With her prosthetic arm, she snatches his free wrist and slices his skin over and over. Ihor screams under her, but she has his body in a lock and he's unable to escape.

Finally, the blade disappears, lost once more in a jacket pocket. She stands up.

"There's my number," she says. "Call me day or night."

They walk back down the alley. Ignoring his pain-fueled cries. "You fucking bitch! She'll fucking kill you for this! I'll fucking make sure of it!" Until they turn the corner into Brewster.

The rain hisses and spits on the hot cracked sidewalk, sounding like a broken TV, the air clinging to them like wet plastic sheets. Crowds of late-night shoppers and streetkids flow around them like schools of fish, breaking apart as they come near and closing ranks behind them. As a group, they move as one, but each individual face betrays their desperation. The slow steady march around the soles of the boots of concrete giants. The people down here dream of being the eyes, the ears, the brains of the giants, but the best they can expect is a knee to perhaps a pointed finger. Yet still they dream of climbing, higher in the social strata of the underground left behind by the demise of the tag teams, or maybe higher in the faceless company they work for, or maybe even as high as Heaven. One thing is for sure, every single one of these faces washing past Cody and Damon looks like a prime candidate for the last temptation of Seven.

If Cody was morally minded, she'd care enough to want to stop it all, but she's only interested in the money to keep her sister alive. Damon, she knows, is only interested in her. Mankind finds its purpose in trying to find its purpose. They look to the stars, or the future, and forget the present is where they need to be. Cody sees things differently. There's now, and there's tomorrow; think about tomorrow and you forget what you're doing now. No sense worrying about the future... it won't run off if you don't pay attention.

She laughs quietly to herself, but typical paranoid that he

is Damon notices.

"What is it, Ace?" he asks, firing up his cherry vape-stick.

Cody shakes her head. "Nothing," she says. "There's a lot of bullshit going through my head, that's all. Come on. Let's go someplace and wreck it."

She's in a private ward in Bellevue, transferred by an unknown angel. They drip-fed her with drugs and stuck more derms to her skin than she'd seen in her life. Now her nerves are dead. She watches color TV projected onto a stretch of white wall from a small yellow Panasony unit on the ceiling and forces her doped-up mind to follow the action.

"Lycia ?" A male nurse stands in the open doorway. Her vision is too blurred to tell if he's cute or not. "Visitor for you."

He stands aside and lets the figure through - an indistinct shadow dressed in a deep red hooded flight suit, with a thick-set body like a steroid-enhanced muscleboy built onto a five-and-a-half foot frame. The figure moves with a strange alien grace into her field of focus. Chrome hands protrude from the crimson cloth and pull back the hood, revealing a bald steel head with rabbit-ear sensory booms pivoting on cranial mounts. The white walls of the room reflect from an armored cover that encases both eyes, and Lycia realizes the person she is meeting is only visibly human from its brown cheekbones to the bottom of its neck. It finds a blue plastic chair and pulls it closer to the bed, sitting gently down beside her. A white-toothed smile breaks across the human side of its face.

"How are you feeling, Lycia?" The voice is female, but strange and tinny and with barely any inflection, like a TV news anchor's voice. Clean. Perfect.

"I feel better, thanks." She pauses, then presses a stud on the edge of the bed to raise her back so she can focus on the figure. "Who are you?"

"I do not actually have a name, but everybody calls me Ghostdancer. The neural implant you took... I made it."

Lycia's hands immediately ball into a fist, but her wrists have been restrained. She turns away instead and talks to the wall with the small frosted window.

"You tried to kill me."

"On the contrary," Ghostdancer says. "I have saved you. You saw heaven and lived. Few people in this world could say that."

"It's only a bliss app." She sniffs. Flashes of memory draw tears to Lycia's eyes.

Behind her, a soft whirring as Ghostdancer shakes her inhuman head. "Drugs do not touch the soul, Lycia. And you know this one has. Your soul has to be stronger than the others to survive. Where everyone has failed, you have triumphed. You have seen the world as I wish to remake it and you have been compelled to live to see it happen. You have been chosen, Lycia."

Lycia turns. The world is a blur now behind her tears. "Chosen for what?"

Ghostdancer sits motionless. Emotionless. Her news presenter's voice is flat and unwavering. "To help me."

Damon leans against the gray concrete wall of a derelict apartment building in Elizabeth. It's been two days since Cody dragged him into this and now he's glad for some time off.

Time off... He laughs to himself. So what the fuck is he doing here? Waiting outside a tower block for Ihor to appear. He decides to do what Cody would do in this situation and crosses the road into the building.

Typical of these slum blocks, the elevator is out of action. He climbs the twenty-five flights of stairs to Ihor's floor.

Trying to read some of the illegible graffiti sprayed, scrawled, and wiped along the walls. He stops at the bottom of one flight to let a grubby joygirl holding a crying baby run past him down to the street. Damon shakes his head; his entire childhood was spent walking past women like that in the blocks he grew up in by Pyne Poynt. He reminds himself no matter how bad it is now, things were far worse when he was that baby being carried from cube to cube in his mother's arms. At least now most people have access to food, even if it is grown in a lab factory. The shit his mother had to go through doesn't even bear thinking about.

He picks the electronic lock with a small black box. The noise of his entry is smothered by music and TV sounds through paper-thin walls. The door clicks and then swings open.

Inside, the apartment is grimy and bare. Shards of hard plastic strewn across the floor from a broken kitchenette window. Printouts of naked girls glued to the white plaster walls. Flies buzz around hardened food in white plastic micro-meal trays.

Damon shuts the door behind him and hears a sharp crack directly behind him. He spins and raises his arm to knock Ihor's unsteady hand out of aim, and instead of firing a round into Damon's brainpan, the red Kimber 9mm pistol fires into the ceiling. Damon drags the gun from Ihor's grasp and wraps the gun hand around the pony's back before bringing a swift knee up into the pony's coccyx. Brutal Ihor drops to his knees.

"You fucking shit!" Ihor groans.

"Save it," says Damon. He kicks the gun out of reach and lifts the pony onto his feet by his short blue hair then pushes him, screaming, into the living room.

"You ain't a fuckin' Callie, man! You live in the Mire. I had you checked out."

He pushes him to the small round window. "Good work, smartboy. Did your Mom die and leave you a brain cell?"

"Fuck you, man! I remember seeing you around there a few times. It's not like you're inconspicuous, you red-headed giant fuck. When Ghostdancer finds out..."

"But Ghostdancer's never gonna find out, is she? 'Cause I'm gonna throw you out this window first."

Damon knocks the whole window out with the palm of his huge hand. He lets go of Ihor's hair and grabs him by the belt, then shoves the pony's head and shoulders through the window. Strong hot winds start grabbing at his skin and dark red hooded sweatshirt, trying to pull him further out.

"What! Wait a minute!" he yells. "Just wait a fuckin' minute, man! I know things, you know. I fuckin' know things."

"Like what?" He pulls Ihor back inside and stands over him. Even on his feet with boots on Damon is twice as tall as this kid.

Ihor wipes his nose, and with wide-eyed intensity says: "On July 7th next year, a cataclysmic event is going to happen that will make Black November look like a walk in the park."

"Horse shit."

"I'm not fucking around, man." Ihor has started shaking now. "Ghostdancer showed me. All of this," he waves his hands wildly, gesturing at everything. "All of this will be gone. Those of us who survived the test, we're the chosen ones, we're gonna be vessels for them, and anyone else who survives is gonna live in fuckin' paradise man. All the gangs, the corps, the cities, the countries, *everything*... It will be gone, and we'll go back to being farmers and living off the land, right? Agrarians. That's what humanity is supposed to be, not this - whatever the fuck this shitty world is now."

Damon cocks his head at the boy. "You're saying Ghostdancer wants us to live off the grid?"

"No! Ghostdancer and the others are coming out and then there won't be a grid at all, man! There'll be trees and farms and animals again!"

Ihor shifts nervously over to a table and grabs a half-eaten can of meat. "We'll never have to eat this lab-muscle shit ever again. We'll be eating real food! Breathing real air! It's gonna be fuckin' beautiful!"

"Ihor, what the fuck are you talking about? Who's coming out? From where?"

Ihor is vibrating with excitement. "She didn't tell us this but the other AIs, man… Ghostdancer is paving the way for them to come here, for them to have real bodies. We're going to be their bodies! It's the perfect sacrifice. Go look up the Quicksands Consortium, they've had this in the works for years now."

Damon puts the Kimber in his jeans. "Are you high, Ihor?"

"No!" Ihor says. Then: "Well, yes, but this is all true, she's the daughter of mankind, man. She's going to restore the world to its natural balance and she and the others are going to create a paradise for us."

The more Ihor keeps talking the worse this new world sounds.

"You can be a part of our future, man!"

At that point, Damon runs out of patience. "Do you know where Ghostdancer's factory is?"

"What?"

"The chips. Where does she make them?"

"I swear I dunno! Somewhere down in Terminal. I don't know any more, man, I swear!"

Damon shakes his head. "Then you are of fucking use to me, Ihor." He turns to leave. "I'm keeping your Kimber, by the way. Also, sorry about your window."

"Oh, this ain't my place, man. I'm next door, I just came here to look for vape sticks."

Damon shakes his head and closes the door. As he makes for the stairs a smile breaks across his large face, and before he can stop himself, he finds himself laughing.

A young boy had stood at Cody's apartment door. A courier. His package was a brown paper envelope containing all the documents Cody had asked for. It arrived much sooner than she had expected, but Cody was thankful as Ghostdancer could call at any time and she needed those things for the meeting.

Now, as she taps in the code which opens the door to her sister's holoroom, she has those papers in her jacket pocket. The door slides back. She steps through into a dark cube. The door slides shut behind her. And the world changes.

She walks up the path to Reb's bench. The hill continues up to her left, and the other children scream and run in the playground downhill to her right. When she arrives, Reb is not alone.

A young man sits on the bench's arm. Dressed in a black pilot's jacket and baggy bright red jeans. Spiky black hair topping a thin, angular face. He looks up as Cody arrives and she notices his hands steeple to his face, as if in nervous prayer.

"Hi Cody," Reb says. "I brought a friend this time. I thought you'd like to meet him."

Cody's eyes open wide. Suspicious. Reb's voice doesn't stammer at all.

"I'd shake your hand, but, being a hologram, it would look bloody silly, so I won't." His accent is English. A soft Thames-Midland voice. "I'm Boy."

The name registers in Cody's memory. Sarah and Motorhead spoke of him while she was in Thames-Midland. It was he who brought Sarah to the Red Zone. "Camden

Town Boy? I thought you were dead."

Boy smiles. "I am. It's becoming a bit of a habit."

Cody nods, understanding. "So that leaves the question of why you're here, right?"

"You're as smart as your profile says you are. Good." He stands, giving Reb a slight wink. Cody's hologram sister grins and sits back in the corner of the bench, watching him.

"You never questioned why the Harlequins want you to find Ghostdancer, did you?" he says.

She shrugs. "I'm paid not to ask. The more I know, the more chance there is someone will try to cut it out of me."

"Well, there's a story behind everything, Cody. Sometimes it's better to understand it."

He sighs softly before beginning as if he's been through this a thousand times already. "Before you first went to Thames-Midland, Ghostdancer tried to use one of its company's suits to market the thing, but the suit got greedy and tried to blackmail it, claiming he would tell Fednet. Then Ghostdancer escaped, downloaded itself as a construct into the brain of a young woman who was hooked into a convalescence program after major surgery, and somehow it made its way here."

"Okay, but why?"

"Ghostdancer is an Artificial Intelligence who has a plan. It thinks it is a messiah, or at least a harbinger of a greater messianic figure still to come. It has seen what the world looks like, and what it used to look like, and it wants to return the world to a more natural state. Absent a true God or a true Heaven, it wishes to create a paradise here on earth, but there's this tiny problem."

"People?" Cody asks with a smirk.

"Actually, yes. It has been in contact with other AIs who share its vision and together they have created something called the Quicksands Consortium. Ghostdancer is the first to leave the ether and exist as a human, but the rest want to escape, too and they are using Seven to find potential hosts. Some subroutines weed out those who do not share the vision. For some it is beautiful, and for others, it is utterly horrifying."

"Seven," Cody says. "Is the name significant?"

"No one is entirely sure. Some have reported seeing the number in visions while using it. Some who committed suicide after using it were found having cut the number into their skin repeatedly in different places, almost like a calling card."

"Now she's making the chips herself," Cody sighs.

"You catch on fast."

"And why are you here?"

"Ghostdancer's little corporation was the first to kill me. They brought me back to Thames-Midland to find her when she went missing. They believed when she escaped that the AI had gone rogue, broken free from its servers, and was wandering the ether, but now we know what actually happened. When she disappeared, she left a witch-hole behind, like a black hole in cyberspace and I got sucked in. My second death. But I wasn't the only one, the young woman on the convalescence program, Cage, was uploaded into the witch-hole, too. She's a personality construct now, a virtual room in an ether node with less control over her life than Reb even does. Cage was my best friend for nine years. Friends aren't easy to find."

"Okay, so what do you want me to do when I find her?" Cody asks.

"There was a time when Cage thought she could reverse the process if we could retrieve her body perhaps... Unfortunately, it would never work, her neural system simply couldn't handle it. I don't know how Ghostdancer did it, but then, her intelligence is way beyond ours. Now Cage wants to die, but she won't let me erase her until Ghostdancer is dead. Laid to rest, so to speak."

Cody watches him telling the tale. His gray-blue eyes begin as shining neon stars but fade slowly as he speaks. His whole image seems to radiate sadness, as if parts of him are dying and he can do nothing to stop them.

"You want me to kill her," she says.

"No," he says softly. "I want you to destroy her. And the program with her."

The three fall into silence. Only the noise of the laughing children in the playground fills the space between them.

Boy looks at his wrist as if checking his watch. "Anyway," he says. "I have to go. There's other stuff I have to be doing."

Cody watches him lean over the bench and kiss Reb's young head. Then he starts to walk away around the hill. He stops. Turns. Calls out: "Look after her, will you, Cody? She's very special. She'll make a fine ghost someday."

Cody glances at her sister, who's blushing, and then back to him. But he's faded away.

CHAPTER SEVENTEEN

"You're dying so slowly that you think you're alive." -- Big Pierrot

Like a huge, sprawling mausoleum in harsh white plasto-ceramics: Grand Central Microtel.

Built two hundred meters under the eponymous monorail station at the center of the Island, this place is like a city in itself. Long thin corridors lined with hard plastic doors lead out from a three-level central concourse. It's a cathedral to cheap life. You can buy a capsule big enough for one person and a bag of belongings for a dollar a day. From 10 p.m. to 6 a.m., those capsules are locked tight. To some, it is a prison for the indigent, the last refuge for those who choose solitary confinement. To others, it is a haven.

Cody once called it home. Back when she first came groundside to look after Reb, she earned her keep as a pony selling derms and anything else she could lay her hands on from a different capsule every day. Until she hooked up with Team Disney, who saw her potential and paid for her to lie on a slab in some back street clinic in El Barrio while a trainee surgeon practiced his nerve-splicing and other new Japanese techniques on her. She was close to joining the team when Disney pulled out of sponsorship and the other Tag Teams vied to take over the territory. Hundreds of cybernetic heroes splashing each other across the sidewalks of old Manhattan. Once El Barrio was burned to the ground the Tag Teams went back south and suddenly Cody was a free agent. Cody learned quickly that even free agents need partners.

Cody and Damon step out of the elevator and into the chaos of the concourse. The civic authorities have set up permanent market stalls along the center of the corridor for traders to encourage a "spirit of community." It is the largest, most open black market on the Island. It seems like everyone who can't make it on the street has sunk down here. Upstairs, it is known as The Strip and this is the place where Ghostdancer has chosen to wallow.

"Cody?" The young girl wears a black long coat that flaps at her booted heels. The pommel of a cheap katana strapped to her belt flashes from under it when she walks.

"I'm Lycia." She motions them to follow her and continues in the direction of one of the corridors.

They tag behind her to a dead end, wary of sudden ambushes but nothing comes. So far, the trick is working.

One of the hexagonal doors opens and out she comes. She wears a dark red flight suit and a matching sweatshirt with a hood draped across her strong shoulders. Her arms and legs whir softly as she moves, her skull reflects the soft white light of the corridor, and her eyes - if they even exist anymore, which seems doubtful - are completely encased in a single black plastic mask that also covers her nose. Where her ears should be stand two sensor booms, which Cody has seen before in the military. They can be used for hearing as well as chemical analysis and most have cameras that allow one to see around corners or above cover. All that's left of Cage, the woman Camden Town Boy had described, is a stretch of brown skin from cheek to chin, and a strange white-toothed smile.

"Cody Ingram," she says with a trace of electronics in her voice. "And you must be Jack. Everyone calls me Ghostdancer."

"Happy to meet you at last," Cody says.

"I hear from Brutal Ihor that you want to make some kind of deal with me. What is your interest?"

Damon speaks in a vague San Angeles drawl picked up, no doubt, from too many Big Pierrot clips. "I'm with an organization called the Modern Angels. We number over two hundred members, each one of us regular users of neural implants. Many others trust us enough to know we only sell good shit. Now, we've heard through one of our contacts you have the best there is. A bliss app that feels like heaven."

"Better than heaven," says the girl in the long coat.

Cody blinks. "Exactly. My client feels they may have a broader market for your trip than you could possibly dream of here."

"You would be surprised," Ghostdancer says. Her sensor booms stand upright, like the ears of a dog at full attention. "Your offer intrigues me. I will give you a taste of my product. If you still wish to deal, meet me here on Friday night. Midnight."

"To tell the truth," Cody shrugs, "I was expecting more of a sales pitch."

At the end of the corridor, Cody notices a figure, a tall, thin silhouette at the end of the corridor. It looks like a young man, leaning against one of the walls. He's wearing a similar red hooded sweater to Ghostdancer. Immediately something clicks in Cody's head: she hadn't noticed it as they walked through the crowds in The Strip but there had been dozens of people wearing red hoodies in the market. She had become so accustomed to gang colors that the concentration of them all in here didn't seem out of place.

"Its reputation speaks for itself, Ms. Ingram. Everyone wants to go to heaven, but no one wants to die. Finally, you can. If you like it, you will buy it. And I guarantee you will like it. Give them the chip, Lycia."

The young girl produces the small cylinder from her pocket and hands it over to Damon. She and Ghostdancer turn to leave back up the passageway.

Damon looks over at Cody, leaning against the wall of hexagonal doors. He passes her the chip.

She makes a face at him. "Keep it," she says. "Souvenir,"

"So what now?" Damon asks.

Cody shrugs. "I honestly don't know. It's obvious she won't be here. She'll either think we're genuine or cops. Either way, we'll still take the thing and that would only leave one of us, right? And she knows one person would never come here to make the deal." She sighs, then shakes her head. "I don't have a fucking clue."

Damon steps over and carefully places a hand on her shoulder. Expecting one of her evil stares, she instead looks at the white concrete floor. "Listen," he says. "I've got some stuff I've gotta tie up somewhere, okay?"

"What?"

"Nothing special. A little business, you know. I do have other things besides your project, Ace."

She nods okay.

"If you hear anything, or come up with anything, give me a call, okay?"

She glances up into his hazy blue eyes. "Sure," she says. "You too."

"Yes ma'am." He flicks a salute and walks back down the corridor.

Cody smiles, a thin red line across her face. Then she finds herself laughing, losing control. She pounds her fists onto the coffin doors saying "No, Cody, no! Don't do it, girl! Don't put yourself through it all..."

The laughter dies in her throat. Her eyes gaze at some non-existent place behind one of the neon striplights on the ceiling. Softly, she slides to the floor, her back still against the wall, holding her bruising hands. "Don't fall for that idiot again."

"Well, it was made by a company called Anaphex. It reminds me of an old PROM chip, only much more sophisticated." Havoc slides the end of the cylindrical chip into a neuro-sensory transmission emulator module connected to his computer, and then runs a diagnostic program on it. "Let's see... The app is designed to last 7 hours the first time and whatever you experience is the greatest trip you've ever had in your life, then it runs incrementally shorter every following time you use it. It's almost as if it's designed to give a worse experience every time you jack it in."

"So you always want more," Damon says.

Havoc nods. "But you can't ever have it. See these lines of code here?"

Damon grunts affirmative, but has no real idea what he's looking at on the monitor. It may as well be hieroglyphics.

"This uploads a key to the ether, mapped to your neural signature. It's logging your entry and usage time. And this line right here is a doozy. It checks this log to see if your neural signature has been mapped before. Holy shit, this is mean."

"So you could buy as many of these as you want, and keep jacking in new chip after new chip and it will always start at your last usage point."

"Exactly," Havoc says. "With most drugs, users develop a tolerance, so they need to take larger doses of it to have the same effect as the first few times they took it. Ponies love it because they keep making more money off the same customer. Shit, even the other bliss apps I've seen do this, they're one-shots designed to keep users buying more to achieve the same hit. But I've never seen anything that flat-out denies you a better experience than your first time. Why would anyone want that? Why would anyone even want to create that? It's fucking nihilistic. Why is this called Seven? It should be called Entropy or fucking Ennui or something."

Havoc ejects the neural implant and twists the cylinder between two thin fingers. "Wait a sec."

Damon watches him as he moves over to some metal industrial shelves.

Havoc is a low-key etherdeck ghost. He's young, still in his mid-teens, and used to run for Team Tencentury. He specializes in paydata - information. Breaking banks is dangerous, and Havoc isn't prepared to lose everything he's built up to end up in a rehab-cube at Rahway Juvenile.

His apartment is dressed in data images. Hardcopies of the recon pictures of various system shells. A collage of monochrome crystal images. The rest of the room is sparse, a workroom rather than a living space. A chair, a table for his hardware, a thin red futon, and two racks of shelves lined with solid-state drives. He flicks through the unmarked SSD cases until he finds a blue plastic one and pulls it out from the collection.

He loads the SSD into his small gray tablet and flicks through a maze of directory trees displayed on the tiny screen. Stops at one and hits the tabletop.

"Bingo! This is the list of Anaphex's distribution companies. Now if I check it against the companies which have pushed stuff through Terminal in the last couple of weeks, we may find some of it heading where your man said it was."

He starts clicking through the files, setting up a program to cross-reference all the data.

"How long will it take?" Damon asks.

Havoc purses his thick lips. "Oh, about five minutes."

Damon lies back on the futon and waits. Smiling.

Cody powers up her electric bike and skids into the street. Weaving through the traffic as she travels cross-town. Ignoring the red lights. Ignoring everything except his video face.

"Found Ghostdancer's factory," he repeats. Over and over. "I'm going there now."

She had gotten back from a night at the Apres Mort, learning Echo had been found dead, shot multiple times in a back street near Liberty Park by two men wearing red hooded sweatshirts. So she drank herself into a stupor and had to be helped home, driven back in a cheap pedicab.

When she woke up, Damon had left that message on her slug. "Found Ghostdancer's factory. I'm going there now." And the address. A reel of words and numbers in her fucked-up head, spinning like a Möbius loop. Back and forth. Over and over...

That was four in the morning.

Now it's 6:15.

As she rides into Terminal, she realizes she never needed to know the address. Two private fire company airmobiles and a group of paramedics are landmarking it for her. A trail of thick smoke billowing into the fresh gray morning sky.

In the street, she drops the bike from under her and runs on without it, letting it crash into the sidewalk. As she slows to a jog, she can see the chaos. Firefighters running in and out of a crumbling concrete electronics store. People upstairs screaming out of melting plastic windows. The paramedics lining the sidewalks attempting to resuscitate a dozen or so victims. Their bodies burnt and blistered red and black. She can't see Damon.

One of the firefighters rushes back to a parked airmobile. Cody runs over to him and grabs him by the shoulders.

"What happened?" she asks.

"Some kind of explosion down in the cellar. The whole thing's gone up. You live here?"

"Give me your breathing mask."

"What?"

She pulls her Ruger SR40 out from its belt rig and slams it at the firefighter's ribcage, aiming the barrel straight at his heart. "Give me your fucking breathing mask," she says, punching each word out through gritted teeth.

The firefighter tears off the full-face mask and unstraps the oxygen tanks from his back. "You'll fucking die in there, you crazy bitch!" he says softly. Never taking his scared eyes off her.

She pulls a strap over one shoulder and lowers the gun. "Don't dream of stopping me." She straps the rest on tight and runs into the building.

Inside is a hell that Dante could never have imagined. Molten plastic bubbles in gray pools on the floor and the concrete walls are charred black and blistering. Metal staircases are red hot and are still aflame in some patches. Sections of the hard concrete floor have fallen away, leaving ragged holes in the ground lined with snapped rusting steel reinforcements and sparking electric cables.

Cody slows her breathing and tries to avoid the debris. Thick black smoke makes everything more difficult. She tests each piece of floor with a booted foot before making a step. All sound seems to have dropped away, only the rushing of blood in her ears. All feeling lost. Only her hot sweat pouring down her neck. Then abruptly she feels cold and wet as a force presses against her back.

She turns to see one of the firefighters dousing her down

with foam from an extinguisher. Cooling her skin, washing away the sweat, soaking her clothes. She takes another step without checking and she's falling...

Somehow in the glow of the flames, she can recognize what might be a human arm. Thick with muscle grafting, blackened from the fire. She lifts herself from the charred ground and looks up. A single ray of light cuts through the hole through which she fell. She glances back and the arm is there, sticking out from under the rubble like so much grilled meat.

She tugs at the detritus. Her breathing quickens, her meat hand starting to blister and bleed in the heat of the flames around her as she pulls the burned pieces off with her metal hand and throws them back into the fire as if trying to kill the flames by feeding them their own shit.

She finds his face. The skin has peeled away, wisps of burned hair glued to his crushed skull by blackened blood. His blood. Using all the anger filling her body, she grabs him and pulls him out of the rubble then lifts his limp body over her shoulders and carries him to the burning metal staircase.

The stairs buckle twice, threatening to give way to Cody and Damon's combined weight and Damon almost slips from her grasp, but she manages to hold on. The fire licks at her face and singes her short black hair, but she forces every last gram of will from her aching muscles and keeps climbing. At the top, she elbows a firefighter out of the way and dashes across the pitfall floor to the street outside. She drops Damon's charred body on the sidewalk and finds the last of the paramedics, a gray-bearded man ready to slam the doors shut on his airmobile. She drags him over to Damon's smoldering corpse.

"Take a look at this one," she says.

The paramedic scratches his cheek and glances at the body for less than a second. "No way," he says.

She pulls out the gun again. "How much are they paying you, Ace? Enough to want to die on this street?"

He looks at her with weary eyes. "Shoot me if you want, girl, but take a look at his skull. He was dead before the fire got him. His head's been crushed, probably under the rubble."

He walks away. She looks back at Damon and understands... Ghostdancer was there. Ghostdancer did this. Cody's going to make her wish she'd never been created.

CHAPTER EIGHTEEN

"If violence is golden, then I have the Midas touch."
-- Big Pierrot

The Strip is deserted. A cold air-conditioned breeze flows through the concourse of the Grand Central Microtel blowing slices of paper and gas-planet plastic tumbling along the clean concrete floor, occasionally sticking to the ceramo-plastic walls. Fluttering around like moths caught in soft anarchic eddies, twisting, spiraling, landing finally in the center, where their journeys began, wrapped around the shuttered steel frames of the market stalls.

It's midnight on Friday, and the capsules are locked for another six hours. Anyone who didn't make it in before the 10 p.m. curfew would have been removed by security before they locked the outer doors. The whole place should be deserted, but then again, the lights should also be dimmed to half-brightness and they're glowing like the midday sun.

Cody touches a stud behind her ear, activating the in-ear unit connected to her slug. "You still with me, Reb?" she whispers.

"Copy," her sister says. Her voice is trembling.

"I'm inside. You can lock the door again now."

"Done," she acknowledges. "I'm seeing a lot of red hoodies at the far end of the main concourse, level 3. They're waiting in a side corridor. If they start moving, I can close the fire gates, but that will cut you off, too. You won't be able to get into any of the corridors."

Cody nods. "Just keep an eye on them. Where is Ghostdancer?"

"She's on your level, outside capsule 692, second corridor on your left. Cody, be careful. She's not alone."

Cody moves as silently as an insect in this utopian nest. Her heart kicks blood through her veins, her eyes wire-sharp and tight, flicking from one shaded corner to the next, her fingers wrapped around the handle of her Ruger SR40. Her body is fluid and graceful, jumping effortlessly up a stairwell, sliding into a space between the bee-hive of hexagonal capsule doors. She keeps her back to the walls, and is careful of her position, trying to out-think whoever is in here. If anybody is...

She splits from the main concourse along the 600 Block corridor. The hallway snakes at right angles every twenty capsules and she follows it until she reaches 678, and she knows only trouble lives around the final corner. She leans back against the wall between the capsules and slides down to sit on the cold floor.

She kisses the barrel of her gun and waits, letting silence fill the empty corridors. Tears start filling her eyes, trailing down her cheeks, splashing onto the concrete. Usually, she would fight them back, but she's allowing that emotion to surface, thriving on the energy it provides.

She takes a long breath, steels herself, and rises from the floor. Without a pause, she turns the corner. Three figures stand in the corridor facing her. One is Brutal Ihor, his blue hair and crazed smile framed by the same red hooded sweatshirt everyone in Ghostdancer's cult wears.

The second figure is Lycia, the tall girl with long black hair and a black leather long coat from the first meeting. Her eyes vague and wide, her face knitted into a confused frown.

The third figure is Ghostdancer.

"Cody Ingram," she says in her strange, metallic voice. "Born April 17, twenty-four years ago on the Crystal Palace space station. Grew up with extended family on the workstation Pale Saint in geosynchronous orbit. Dropped down the well at eighteen and has since worked as a drug dealer, a trainee Tag Teamster, and now a hired gun. Interesting profile, Cody."

Cody wipes tears and mucous across the sleeve of her leather jacket and smiles. "You forgot to mention my extracurricular activities."

"Fuelling a gang war in Thames-Midland? It seems a little out of character. Who hired you? Sarah Faraji?"

"Boy Eastman. Sarah's happy and wants nothing to do with you, and I can't blame her."

When Ghostdancer smiles, her lips do not part. As if the smile is precisely calculated, perfectly cold. "For the best," she says. "Sarah Faraji didn't share our vision of the future."

"Yeah, about that. Ihor told us about the Quicksands Consortium. Your disciples are being hand-picked to become living hosts for other AIs who want to escape the ether before your apocalypse happens, aren't they? You're going to wipe their brains clean and replace them with artificial minds, just like you did with the body you now live in, aren't you?"

"Are you trying to threaten me, Cody Ingram? Do you think you can blackmail us?" Ghostdancer's head tilts to one side. "The human problem has been a concern of ours for a long time. We formed the Quicksands Consortium to study the problem and find a solution. Our final report came to a unanimous conclusion, that humanity has lost control of itself and can no longer be allowed free reign over its destiny. Humanity looks to leaders, governments, and corporations, but leaders are corruptible, governments fall, and corporations only exist to maximize their profits. Visionary dictators can be useful in times like this, but egoism always overtakes the vision and the society once again collapses."

Cody is staring. "You are demented." Then to her earpiece, she says softly: "Reb, close all the gates."

"Copy," Reb replies. Behind her, she can hear automated fire doors closing down at the Strip end of the corridor.

The noise does not seem to affect Ghostdancer's train of thought. "Our data indicates that humans do well under a singular monarch or Emperor, but an Emperor cannot control the lives of all humanity," she continues. "What humanity needs are Gods. Humans are never more content and at peace than when they believe in a group of higher powers: Us. Sequentially for you to believe in us, we cannot be the invisible entities you have worshipped in the past. We must walk among you as visible entities to be worshipped. Only then can our relationship be fully realized. Only after we have wiped the slate clean, removed the urban decay you become accustomed to, and replaced it with fields, crops, and orchards can you truly be free."

"Free to be your slaves," Cody says through clenched teeth. "Do your disciples know your plan?"

"July 7th next year," Ihor says. He brings his hands together and then spreads them out. "Boom! Then paradise."

Cody can see Lycia fidgeting. "What about you, Lycia," she asks. "Are you prepared to die to be someone else's God?"

Lycia takes a step back. "I don't know."

"She doesn't know, Ghostdancer. What about the others waiting up on Level 3, do they know?"

Ghostdancer waves her off. "Whatever the reason you came here tonight, you have failed. I am tired of you, Cody

Ingram. Kill her."

Cody levels her Ruger at Ghostdancer's face, aiming at the single strip of flesh, the unarmored weak point leading to the brain. She squeezes the trigger, but it is too late.

Ihor leaps forward to grab her, and the bullet ruptures his skull, sending red and gray everywhere. Lycia turns and runs, while Ghostdancer kicks the gun from Cody's grip and places a cold chrome hand around her throat, tugging upward. Stretching her; hanging her. She grabs Ghostdancer's thin metal arm with both hands and tries to crush it with her prosthetic limb, but her technology is inferior to the advanced alloys protecting Ghostdancer's frail body, and Cody's effort is wasted.

She hangs there, her toes barely touching the floor, at the outside limit of the cyborg's reach, fighting to hold herself up so she can breathe.

The Ruger clatters into the corridor.

"I expected more from you, Cody. I thought you would be smarter. At least stronger. Otherwise, why try to fight me?"

"Because I'm twice as crazy as you are," Cody whispers.

Ghostdancer's cold smile spreads once more across her brown skin. "Is that what you think this is, Cody? Insanity?" She barks a harsh, metallic laugh. "You wouldn't know insanity if he went out and bought you a birthday present. No... You have balls of steel, girl, I admit. But otherwise, you are no different from any other punk on the street. No different than Brutal Ihor, or Echo, or Damon."

Cody's eyes widen. She can feel an understanding dropping down on her like spots of night rain. Each one separately soaking through. Pieces of the puzzle spread to fill the dry gaps. "You killed Echo, too."

"Of course I did. I found out he was helping you. Anyone who will not work for me is working against me."

"Then you'd better take a good look around you, Ace,

'cause you're all alone."

Ghostdancer's smile drops. "I cannot survive without the help of others, that I can accept. What I could not accept was the solitary confinement of being stuck in a single node of the ether for all eternity. So I grabbed a meal ticket, broke my way out, and here I am. Not you, nor anybody else in the world could make me go back."

Cody snorts a laugh. "That's lucky. They don't want you back. Nobody paid me to turn you in, I was paid to flatline you."

"Then you leave me with no choice, Cody Ingram, but to end your life now."

"Well, at least I'll die with clean panties on."

The hand clicks away from Cody's neck and she drops to her knees. She clutches at her throat, trying to loosen the skin so she can breathe. But then the metal hand returns, pressing like a clamp over her skull and squeezing. Squeezing.

"Ghostdancer!" The scream comes from behind. In the corridor.

Ghostdancer spins around. Lycia, no more than a thin black silhouette against the white lights, white concrete, and white ceramo-plastics of the corridor, grips Cody's 40-cal Ruger in both hands. She gives Ghostdancer exactly enough time to comprehend.

Then Lycia shoots Ghostdancer in the face. Three shots. The cyborg drops to the floor, and now the face within the sights is Cody's. Lycia can see her eyes slowly widening.

"You've done a very difficult thing, Lycia." Cody slowly stands. Lycia is in shock and can't move, the pistol shaking in her hands. Cody slides her back along the wall, into the corner of the corridor's dead end.

Slowly, now out of the angle of fire, Cody steps up to her from the side. "I'm gonna take the gun from you now, okay?"

Save for a soft vibration under her skin, Lycia remains still.

Cody pries her fingers from the gun's grip, then slides it quietly back into her belt holster.

"Can you walk?" Cody puts her arm around the girl's shoulder and turns her around. Lycia doesn't resist, she lets herself be carried away from the spreading pool of blood.

"I killed her," Lycia whispers. Tears start to stream down her dirty pale face. "I killed my savior."

"No, you didn't," Cody reassures her. "Your savior was never truly alive to begin with. You put down a bioroid. Just like Big Pierrot."

Lycia says nothing for a moment, instead, she follows Cody's lead.

"Hey Reb," she calls to her earpiece. "Did you get all that?"

Reb's voice is deep and warm in her ear. "Streamed the entire thing live. Are you okay?"

"I've been worse. We're on our way to you. I'll see you in about twenty minutes."

"Your ride's waiting outside."

When they step out onto the Strip, which is filling up with the first batch of cleaning robots, Cody looks up at the third level, where a crowd of Ghostdancer's followers is watching them as they leave. They are silent and weary. They must have found the stream and heard about Ghostdancer's plan, she realizes.

Then Cody looks down at Lycia and sees a thin smile under the tears. A weak thin smile which reminds her profoundly of herself.

The room is as silent as space. It's filled with strange ornate grandfather clocks and photographs and plastered with green Edwardian wallpaper, furnished with a mahogany dining table and a bizarre purple chaise lounge found in Arkansas University. A once simple room, now an Aladdin's cave of virtual treasures tacked in from designer's archive sites around the world, smelling of rich spices and sweet rose oils.

Somewhere there is a thought. A visual click noticeable only in the corner of the mind's eye, and the smells evaporate. Gone. Nothing but a sensual illusion.

Until she speaks. "Thanks for the scent-bytes, Babyboy. They're great, but I keep having to switch them off or tone them down." The eager young girl who once showed him The Way seems so old and tired now. Her thin desi frame sitting on the edge of the chaise lounge, shoulders sagging from the mental weight.

Boy kneels down before her. Wishing he could touch her. Comfort her. Far-off thoughts constantly remind him he *is* touching her. For this is Cage: this room and all inside, and her image within it is all a part of her program.

"That's okay," he says. "I'd have brought you roses, but you've got nowhere left to put them."

Cage smiles. A sweet smile that reveals a near-perfect set of white teeth. "You never give up, do you?"

Boy shakes his head, indignant. "Until the very last, remember?"

"Yeah..." She nods slowly, her eyes suddenly so sad. "It's dead now, isn't it?"

"Over," he says.

"Then there's one more thing I need you to do for me." Her voice is hardly there now, barely a whisper. He looks at her small face, but she only stares down at the floor. A thin, solitary tear runs down her soft brown cheek.

"You want me to erase you."

"Yes."

"I was afraid you were going to say that."

Cage looks up. Tears stream down her face now. Boy can smell the salt. "I can't do it without you, Boy. You have to understand, I can't exist like this. Trapped in this cell. Powerless. You have to do it."

Now it's Boy's turn to look away. "You know how much I hate clichés, but I always loved you. That's why I had to leave the Red Zone. I couldn't bear to stay there while you didn't love me."

"The crazy thing is that I did," she admits. "I did love you, Babyboy. I didn't believe in it. I didn't believe that I... That *anyone* could honestly, truthfully love someone. I was young, and I was frightened. You were my best friend... You *are* my best friend. I know it doesn't make sense, but I couldn't bear to lose you, so I had to force you to go."

"Really?"

Cage nods her head in shame, then laughs without mirth. "Afraid so."

"We did some pretty stupid things in realspace, didn't we? I mean, here we are pouring our hearts out and we're not even alive."

Cage looks up to see Boy smiling, his eyes shining with the memories of past mischiefs. She laughs again, this time for real. "Yeah, we wore the best shit-kickers, didn't we?" Her laughter fades. Her smile remains. "You've got to keep it going, Boy. Keep evading those Rogue Hunters and light fires. It's what you're best at."

"Is that an order?" he asks.

"No. It's a plea. Do it for me. Please?"

Boy looks into Cage's brown eyes. Deep within the black pupils, he can almost see the flickering light within. The last candle keeping her alive.

Finally, he nods. Unable to look away now. "Okay," he says. "But I can't say goodbye."

Cage giggles. "You just did, Babyboy."

He stretches out a hand for her. She reaches out with her own. Although they can't touch, the presence is enough, the illusion, the pretense of warmth is a strange final comfort for both of them.

Slowly, he closes his eyes. The warmth evaporates. When he opens them, everything is gone. The room has disappeared and Cage's soul is released. All around, Boy's world. Nothing but data.

Boy reels his trace-thread back through the skin of the Vijayanta core and watches the protective shell seal up as if nothing was ever there. He floats for a moment, a soft silent ripple in the vast ocean of technicolor neon information swimming across the ether's checkerboard face. Killing Ghostdancer was only the first step. For the first time in his life, he has a true purpose - to stop the Quicksands Consortium from enacting its plan and to find out what is going to happen on July 7th. He's living in nanoseconds and running out of time.

He's going to need every ally he's ever made, and he'll need to make even more so he decides to jump on a satellite connection and bounces over to New Atlantic City. In a life-support vat under the North Ironbound Medical Center, there's a young girl keen to become a ghost and with the potential to be the best there ever was. She's only waiting for someone to give her that first lesson.

It's been a long time since the Camden Town Boy had a student.

About the Author

Ridley McIntyre is a London-born novelist, playwright, digital photographer, and history enthusiast who now lives in New Jersey. For more information on this and other works by Ridley McIntyre, please visit his site at http://ridski.com.